All
Rights
Reserved
for You

All Rights Reserved for You

Sudeep nagarkar

EBURY
PRESS

EBURY PRESS

USA | Canada | UK | Ireland | Australia
New Zealand | India | South Africa | China

Ebury Press is part of the Penguin Random House group of companies
whose addresses can be found at global.penguinrandomhouse.com

Published by Penguin Random House India Pvt. Ltd
7th Floor, Infinity Tower C, DLF Cyber City,
Gurgaon 122 002, Haryana, India

First published in Ebury Press by Penguin Random House India 2016

ISBN 9788184007435

Typeset in Adobe Garamond by Manipal Digital Systems, Manipal
Printed at Replika Press Pvt. Ltd, India

www.penguinbooksindia.com

To the love of my life,
my wife—
Jasmine Sethi

Though I am a writer, she is the one who completed
my love story!

Prologue

It was the month of July, 2015. Everyone was hooked to the popular show *Game of Thrones*. Those who weren't watching it were relegated as aliens. The Indian web series TVF Pitchers, created by The Viral Fever, was bringing unusual, innovative content to the small screen, but there was still a section of the population that preferred back-to-back episodes of *CID* and *Savdhaan India* on television on a lazy Sunday morning.

Prime Minister Modi had launched the Digital India programme to simplify our problems and make the country digitally empowered. But our lives still revolved around the controversial blue ticks on WhatsApp, and whether our friend or foe had 'read' our messages or not. However, the problems of the real world trumped those of the digital world by a mile. Real-life problems, like introducing your girlfriend to your parents, still scared the shit out of boys.

'No, I don't want to be a part of this plan!' she exclaimed.

'Trust me, it'll work. We can pull it off,' I pleaded.

I knew that we were technically trying to commit suicide by planning to land up at my house without prior intimation and introducing her as my girlfriend to my parents. Would you deem it any less than a suicide attempt?

We were at Starbucks with our friend Dipika and her younger sister, Roma, when I decided to call my parents. I didn't want to give them too many details but thought it best to let them know we were coming. I went outside the restaurant to make the call so that I could talk to them without being disturbed.

The call took more than a minute, and when I came inside, I could see the anxiety on my girlfriend's face. As she flashed me a worried smile, I decided to calm her down by holding her hand. 'They have asked us to come home in an hour,' I muttered.

'But what did you say to them?' she asked with a raised eyebrow.

'I said that I wanted to introduce them to a very special person in my life.'

'Are you insane? Who on earth does something like this? Fuck, you screwed everything up.'

'I didn't. Believe me,' I reassured her.

I tried to console her, unsure about the outcome of the meeting myself. My head was filled with ifs and buts. At that moment I thought about how much impact she had had on my life. I wasn't even fully aware of the effect she had on me. After three years of being in a long-distance relationship, we had finally decided to take things to the next level, only to realize that it wasn't as easy as it had seemed.

Eventually, I was overwhelmed with more questions than answers. I thought to myself, *Is there a difference between just spending all your time together and being married?*

Yes, there is, I realized. Once you tie the knot, the whole dynamic of the relationship changes. The degree of love and affection that you share intensifies immensely.

Looking at her, I thought, *What did I do to deserve her? Gosh, I'm a lucky man!*

We never bothered with what others thought about us because only we could understand how much we meant to each other. Having a partner who understands you without you having to say anything is the best feeling in the world.

This was one of the most critical days of our lives as it would decide what lay ahead for us. It was more critical for her as a girl, since her life would go through a complete transformation if everything went according to plan.

Girls who pretend it's not such a big deal are the ones who are most affected by it. Putting up a strong front is a defence mechanism for them. She too stayed calm in front of us and didn't let on about the turbulence within her.

The four of us drove to my house. Before ringing the doorbell, I hugged her and kissed her forehead to assure her that no matter what the outcome, we would face it together.

My mom opened the door and welcomed us in. I tried to read her face to understand what was going on in her head. But I drew a blank. She led us to the drawing room where Dad was sitting, reading the paper.

After casual introductions, we sat on the plush sofa. I could gauge the nervousness on her face. She deliberately did not sit next to me, instead choosing a spot at the far end of the sofa, next to Dipika.

Although we had come well prepared, all our preparation vanished into thin air. We sat for a while in silence, waiting for someone else to break the ice.

'Are you already married or what?' Dad questioned.

'Dad?' I had an annoyed look on my face.

'When you called to tell us about your "special someone", we thought you were coming home directly after a court marriage. So how did you two meet? What's your story?'

Holy shit! His response was totally unexpected. We were not at all prepared for this. At that moment, I felt like a student who had prepared all the chapters for his viva except one, only to find the professor asking questions from that very chapter.

She kept quiet and looked at me nervously. My father soon slipped from English into his mother tongue Marathi. Being Punjabi, she could barely understand our conversation, and that made her feel even worse, as she didn't know how to respond or what was expected of her. Everything seemed alien to her—the place, the language, the people. I looked at her to reassure her that I had everything under control. I took a deep breath and narrated our story.

'We met at a bookstore for the first time. Her friend's father owned the bookstore. I got her address through a register the bookstore maintained of all its visitors and sent her a love letter via post, not in the least expecting a reply. But she did reply! Gradually, in the process of exchanging letters, our feelings for each other grew. Soon, we met for the first time, and after a couple of such meetings, we realized we were in love.'

As I narrated the story, I could sense from everyone's reaction that they didn't believe us at all. I knew I had made a blunder and realized what a pathetic storyteller I was. I wished I could just unsay what had just been said but that was not an option either. All I could do was nervously wait for my parents to respond.

'Are you sure it's a true story and not make-believe, fiction, like your books?'

'It's the only story I've ever told truthfully,' I concluded, feigning a smile.

A few hours later . . .

Romance prevails only when two people manage to convey that they care for each other through small acts of love and affection. It blooms under the constant affection of the significant other, the one who goes out of their way for the sake of your comfort. I felt the same way when I introduced Jazz to my parents and the smile of contentment on her face told me of her joy.

Jazz was short for Jasmine, a name I had lovingly given her soon after we became a couple. At first, my parents were convinced that our story was anything but true. My feelings for Jazz, however, persuaded them otherwise. Their affirmative nod to our relationship, without any added interrogation on the topic of inter-caste marriages, was rather unexpected. Because, even though we say we live in the twenty-first century where religions, customs and traditions are constantly being updated in order to meet the modern lifestyle, when it comes to marriage, we all know that the situation somehow reverses in the blink of an eye.

Whatever the reason, it surely called for a celebration. Both of us were in good spirits as we headed to Tap Resto Bar in Bandra, along with our dear friends Dipika and Roma.

'Your dad is so cool. And here I was expecting a full-on Hindi melodrama, with your dad donning the scary avatar of Amrish Puri from *DDLJ*! I am so glad he turned out to be Anupam Kher instead,' Dipika joked as I drove past the Bandra Kurla Complex.

'You are such an idiot. At least you should have narrated our story properly,' Jazz added.

'I was clueless. If I had to think about it for even a fraction of a second more than I did, it would have sounded completely fake.'

'But it did sound fake.' Jazz giggled nervously.

'Whatever, you guys. According to me, this first innings in Mumbai went well. Jazz will now have to lead the second innings with her parents in Delhi, so let's see how well she performs.' I winked.

Jazz didn't react and looked out the car window instead. She very well understood that this game was nowhere near over. She was always above orthodox traditions but I could see in her eyes how worried she was about her parents.

With one hand on the steering wheel, I placed the other on her leg. If you can't feel the silence of your partner, you will never understand their words.

She placed her hand on mine and looked at me lovingly. The moment was so intimate and sacred that I wished I could capture and frame it for eternity. In the rear-view mirror, I could see a confused expression on Roma's face. When we asked what was wrong, she said she was still curious about how we met. She knew we hadn't told my parents the whole truth.

We reached the bar and took a table on the rooftop, from where we had a good view of the city, and immediately placed an order for snacks and drinks to celebrate.

'So when are *you* getting married?' I asked Dipika.

'Why does everyone who gets engaged ask the same question? I mean, if you are going to ruin your life, it doesn't mean that the world will follow you to your grave. Rest in peace, Aditya. I will sincerely mourn your death,' Dipika teased.

'I won't let him die so soon. I still have to make optimum use of his credit cards. Until then . . .' Jazz trailed off slyly.

I ignored them and directed my next question at Roma, who still looked like her mind was elsewhere.

'Why are you so quiet?'

'Because I have some questions for both of you. Shall I?'

'Sure, go ahead,' Jazz answered.

'Was it really true . . . all that you told your dad? I want the complete story, if you don't mind reliving it for me,' said Roma.

'The one Aditya narrated to his parents?' Jazz responded, barely being able to conceal her laughter.

'Please tell me the truth. It's killing me. How can it be possible? Letters through post and that too in the age of social media apps? Are you guys retarded or taking up monkhood?' Roma kept bombarding us with questions one after another.

We had told Dipika to keep the finer details of our relationship a secret, and it seems like she had stayed true to her word, not even disclosing the facts to her sister.

No one spoke for several seconds.

'So . . . was all of that true?' she badgered.

'Not at all. The *real* story is something else.' I grinned, taking Jazz's hand in mine.

I shifted my gaze to Jazz, who had probably, in a split second, recollected all the moments that we had lived through. Every relationship requires effort, but a long-distance relationship requires extra effort. One of the greatest surviving myths about long-distance relationships is that they are more likely to fail than any other kind of relationship. However, Jazz and I are a living testament to long-distance relationships making it in the real world!

All you need is a person you can trust, without feeling the need to harbour feelings of obsessive insecurity. I had seen that trust in Jazz, and I was sure she had seen it in me as well, which is precisely why we are where we are today. Of course, I am aware that not all long-distance relationships survive, but I like to believe that they are not any more likely to end in an early demise than any another kind of relationship.

We kept it real from the very beginning, you see. Jazz never made promises that she couldn't keep, neither did she ever lie to me to provide the temporary comfort and satisfaction that lies are notorious for. The one thing that she did was make me believe in myself, that I could be the man with whom she could spend the rest of her life. Coming this far wasn't easy but all our efforts were worth it. Roma continued to stare at us while these thoughts unfolded in my mind. As I took a bite of my meal, I started narrating our story—the real one!

Jazz

'No one is as adventurous as you! God, these stunts will cost you big one day. What thrill do you get out of them? And you've dragged me into one too!' Jazz lamented, as she passed a pair of gloves to him, pulling out another pair from her bag.

'The thrill of flying. Nothing can beat it!'

'Let's see . . .' Jazz said, tying her hair into a ponytail as she prepared herself for the zip-line adventure, the very popular outdoor activity that gives games enthusiasts the adventure and thrill of flying through the air on a zip-line. It is an aerial runway consisting of a pulley suspended on a cable, enabling adventurers holding on to the pulley to move from one point of the inclined cable to the other.

Jazz, a Sikh girl from Delhi, was ambitious, full of life and fiercely independent. Her life was an open book, though she did have a mysterious side. She could add you on Facebook instantly but would give you a hard time if you wanted to be added to her life. She was someone who knew how to speak her mind, someone who could captivate you simply with her words. She had looks to die for but dressed only in outfits in which she felt comfortable and confident. She attracted people towards her naturally and was very different from the girls who dressed up in mini-skirts and shorts just to attract attention.

She never limited herself and was always open to new ideas, places and people. She was someone who didn't need the approval of others to develop a sense of self-esteem, someone whose strong personality made her more than just another pretty face.

'Remember the last two rides? If I win like I have in the past, you will buy me an original Jimmy Choo handbag. Not one from Sarojini Nagar market,' Jazz said.

'And if I win . . . you will buy me a bottle of premium Scotch. So shall we begin?' Randeep said, as he tightened the harness.

Randeep was Jazz's childhood friend. His ultimate aim in life was to apply for a US visa and settle abroad for good. Adventurous, crazy and sociable, Randeep was instantly likeable and a very good friend to Jazz. He knew how to balance his personal and work lives, and he never let one interfere with the other. Like Jazz, he liked living a life of adventure, and zip-lining was one of them. Every alternate weekend, they would try a new outdoor sport and had only very recently become addicted to zip-lining.

'Let's go,' Jazz agreed.

She found her limbs succumbing to the calm serenity of the higher altitude. Gradually, she sat down on the edge of the first zip line and looked down. Her mind roared like a race car at the starting line, ready to take off at any second.

As soon as she felt that she was secure on the harness, she gave Randeep a thumbs up and pushed off.

She had begun picking up speed unusually fast. The surroundings became a blur of motion. What were once trees now merely looked like green trails. Slowly, other colours started invading her vision. Blues and purples zoomed past her as she picked up more and more speed— to the point where she couldn't even distinguish one object from another. Colours flashed in the periphery of her vision. Everything felt ethereal as she recalled the feeling of not believing what she was seeing as she came down with such momentum. She looked over to her right and her entire life flashed before her eyes—she could see herself as a mischievous three-year-old, trying to hide her old crayons under the sofa, so that she could get new ones. To her left, she could see herself finishing elementary school along with her best friend, Randeep.

Before she could brace herself for it, she found herself at a lecture, during which she had received her first love letter. Something she had completely ignored. *This can't be a daydream. I have not passed out*, she thought as she was quite unable to digest the lucidity of her memories. She could now see the zip-line and the harness she was strapped to. Yet such physical strappings did not matter, and memories started flooding her mind as if coming from some kind of omniscient source.

She swirled through her graduation. Her brother was leaving for the US in order to pursue his higher studies. She literally saw him waving his arm at the departure gate as she felt she was picking up more and more speed. The milestones in her life flew past. She was zipping through time.

What happens if I get off this zip line? Will I stay in that specific point in time? What's at the end of this? Where am I landing? Her thoughts swarmed her as she realized that she had halted all of a sudden. She looked down one more time. With each beat, her heart tried to dig its way out of her chest. Her breath was shallow and thick. Just a few moments ago, everything had sped up to a chaos inside her head and now, everything was back to that sullen calmness which had surrounded her before the fall. Randeep was cruising gradually and was still behind her. Jazz hung suspended in mid-air, trying to push herself ahead. The next second, Randeep kicked her with enough force that Jazz finally managed to reach the end. For all their games, she had won for it was she who had reached the end before Randeep. Soon, leaving the plethora of thoughts behind her, she jumped in joy, flashing a victorious smile at Randeep.

Randeep simply patted her back and said, 'You reached your goal only because a good friend like me kicked you so hard, reminding you that you were lost midway.'

Friendship is such a fountain of treasures. Friends who are loyal are always there to make you laugh when you are down, they are not afraid to help you avoid mistakes and they look out for your best interests. Randeep was one such friend who was always there for Jazz, every single time she had been lost and had fumbled in her life. He kicked her and made her believe in herself once again. He was a giver. Such friends are truly hard to find, people who offer a friendship that lasts a lifetime.

'Whatever. You owe me a bag. That's the end of the story,' Jazz stated.

'Okay, okay . . . We will go with Priyanshi. Call her.'

'But where is she?' She didn't answer the last time I called her.'

'She isn't picking up even now. Should we go to her apartment?' Randeep asked.

'With or without Priyanshi, you owe me a bag. Got it?'

Priyanshi

'Where do you work?' the stylist asked.

'I'm preparing for the UPSC exam . . . How is this related to the hair cut?' Priyanshi asked.

'I just wanted to confirm if a fancy hairdo was allowed at your work place.'

'That's not a problem. Can we begin?' Priyanshi asked impatiently as she looked at her wristwatch.

Priyanshi was originally from Guwahati and had made Delhi her current place of residence, since she was preparing for the UPSC entrance exams and all the good coaching centres were in the capital city.

She stayed in Jazz's neighbourhood in a rented apartment. They had befriended each other in a very short span of time and their friendship had soon turned into sisterhood.

Priyanshi was under a lot of stress as her family didn't want her to join the civil services. Secondly, as someone from the North-east, she faced a lot of bullying and eve-teasing on a regular basis, not just at her coaching centre but also on the streets, markets and malls. There was no escaping it.

Priyanshi was a go-getter and would not let any of this get in the way of her dreams. Hard-working and disciplined, she was always engrossed in her books. Yet, every now and then, she found her concentration breached due to the amount of mental stress she had to put up with. She had recently befriended Randeep through Jazz, and often Randeep became her source of moral support.

On that particular day she had decided not to answer any calls because she wanted to concentrate on her appointment with her hairstylist at the salon. Despite having taken an appointment, she had to wait for almost an hour, after which she realized her real ordeal had only just begun. Shampooing, conditioning, one thing followed by another. Every time she assumed that stylist was done with her hair, some other equipment or lotion would pop up before her eyes.

The rapid-fire questions from the hairstylist continued—which hair care products did she use, did she have any chemical allergies, was she a first-time visitor. By then she was rather pissed off and impatient for the scissors to snip her long frizzy strands. But not yet! Out came the clips. Six to the left and six to the right. The auspicious moment of actually cutting her hair arrived only when he was done with the clipping, as if he were deliberately teasing her. But she was careful to remind him about the length because she still wanted to be able to tie her hair in a ponytail. Once he assured her he knew what he was doing, she surrendered her lovely locks to his mercy. After all, he was the style director.

After a few snips, he announced that he was done. He brought her a hand-mirror as if rejoicing in the final effect, his grand finale. She shrieked, looking at herself in the mirror. 'What have you done? You've cut it too short! God, I'm never coming back to this salon again. Fuck you!' she screamed and rushed out.

Her features attracted enough prejudiced attention in public and she didn't want any of it. All this hairstyle did was draw more attention to her. Still conscious of how she looked, she rushed to her apartment, where Randeep and Jazz were waiting for her.

'What the fuck? What have you done to your hair?' Jazz looked shocked.

'Looks like someone cut your hair in their sleep!' Randeep laughed.

Priyanshi gave him an annoyed look, walking fast, her stilettos tapping furiously on the road.

'I don't want to talk about it.'

'Did you go to some B-grade salon to save some money?' Randeep continued teasing her.

'I spent Rs 2500 on this. Can you believe it? My pillow gives me a better hairstyle than this every morning.'

'How can you goof up so badly when you have a friend like Jazz—Ms Fashion Daily?'

Jazz pinched Randeep, warning him to be sensitive towards Priyanshi.

'Who told you to experiment? Change is good but you shouldn't be so risqué about something you are so unsure of,' Jazz said.

Randeep sat beside Priyanshi as he tried to raise her spirits and somehow he succeeded. Sometimes, friends were more than just company. You cannot imagine a life without them. Jazz, Randeep and Priyanshi shared such a bond. Priyanshi was their darling and they always pampered her. All three were completely unlike each other but they liked each other's company nonetheless.

'Who was the one who suggested you treat your hair like a science lab?' Jazz continued with her lecture and interrogation.

'Dipika, my college friend . . . the one you met a few days ago,' Priyanshi replied with a sheepish smile on her face.

Dipika

'Are you alive?' Dipika messaged, as I was lying in bed.

'Nope. I'm a zombie,' I replied just to irritate her.

'*shoots you in the head; then shoots you twice more, just to be sure* :P,' she messaged back.

'Smart move :D,' I replied.

'At least, now you know I'm prepared in case you turn into a zombie.'

'I would do the same for the people I care about.'

'What about the rest?'

'Let them starve outside while I chill in a shelter. Ha ha!' I somehow ended on a higher note.

Dipika finally decided to put an end to it by adding, 'Huh, anyway, can you pick me up? There's no one at home and I am hungry. And I am not a zombie as you know :P'

Dipika was my one true friend, someone who always had my back. We fought very rarely, and what I loved about her was that she would never talk behind your back; if there was an issue, she would always approach you first. She was the kind who loved to give free advice to anyone and everyone, even to those who didn't need any. She also loved to play a lot of pranks, and with her I could be my goofy self without the fear of being judged.

She was very good at keeping secrets and I could trust her with anything. Even cringe-worthy secrets like having peed in a public swimming pool. Obsessed with sitcoms and historical dramas, she maintained a firm belief that those who had not watched a single episode of *Game of Thrones* or *Friends* did not deserve to live in this era and should probably move to another planet.

That's how she befriended Priyanshi, who was also a big fan of *Friends*. They both went to the same college and their love for the show brought them together. Dipika aspired to become a writer and was working on her first manuscript.

When I reached her home, she was all worked up about someone repeatedly calling her.

'There's an agitated lady on the phone and she has mistaken my number for MTNL's complaints number. She keeps calling me again and again despite the fact that I've repeatedly informed her that she has dialled the wrong number! I think I'll have to report her to the police. I won't have anyone disturb me when my favourite show is on,' Dipika complained as she hung up and played an episode of *Friends* on her laptop.

The phone rang again. Dipika put it on loudspeaker.

'Hello? MTNL? Listen, don't play games with me. Okay? I know this is the right number. Don't try to avoid me. Do you know who I am?' the lady at the other end screamed.

'Welcome to MTNL's automated fault-booking service. To continue in English, press one.'

Beep. The lady had actually pressed one on her dial pad. Dipika gave me an evil grin and continued with her instructions, in a robotic voice.

'To register a complaint, please enter the last five digits of your driving licence number after the beep. BEEP.'

We could actually hear the lady furiously rummaging through her bag looking for her driving licence. She seemed to have found it pretty fast as we heard the following beeps.

'Because of the spam we have been receiving, we will now perform a check to see if you are human. Please enter the result of thirty-nine multiplied by five divided by eleven.'

We could hear the lady shouting out to someone in the background and asking for an answer. The person asked why she needed it and the lady added, 'I'm registering a complaint for our dead phone.' The guy in the background naturally sounded extremely confused but the lady ignored this and insisted on getting an answer to the question.

'Err . . . it's . . . ah . . . fourteen point . . . errr . . .'

Beep-beep.

The lady pressed two buttons on her dial pad.

'Your complaint has been registered. Thank you for calling MTNL,' Dipika concluded the conversation.

At the other end, we could hear how pleased the lady was. To the person in her background, she screamed that MTNL had become so high-tech that they did not even need to register the number of their dead landline and then she disconnected.

'Somehow, when you pull stunts such as these, you fuel the myth of writers being a jobless species.' I giggled.

'I am not a writer yet.'

'You'll soon be one.'

She was unsure of her writing abilities and wanted to get some recognition to prove herself.

According to her, I was doing decently well as a writer, but to my relatives and outsiders, I was still jobless as I worked from home, unlike others who were out of the house and at their respective offices before I even woke up.

As we ordered food, Dipika excused herself to go to the bathroom but left her phone on the table. I am always curious when it comes to what's going on in my best friend's life. I opened her Facebook Messenger and toggled through her recent chat with Priyanshi. I found a group picture of Dipika, Priyanshi and some girl I didn't recognize. Before I could investigate any further, I saw Dipika come out of the bathroom. I immediately put her phone aside and pretended to scroll down my own Facebook newsfeed. To my shock, the same photograph that I had just seen popped up on my newsfeed, apparently shared by Dipika herself. The unfamiliar girl had caught my attention. I stopped scrolling and tapped on the picture, zooming in and out. The girl in the picture had kohl-black hair which fell heavily to her sides, covering her shoulders. She had a decanter-shaped waist and her complexion was an impeccable shade of peach. Her pencil-thin eyebrows arched over her sweeping eyelashes. A sculptor could not have fashioned her any better. Never before had temptation been so strong for me. The only thing I wanted was to know all about her! Somehow! Anyhow!

Relationship Signal Strength: Strong

Mumbai

The moment I reached home, ignoring all my work and without even bothering to change my clothes, I opened her Facebook profile on my laptop because I wanted to see her clearly in a large picture with good resolution and not as a tiny image on my mobile screen.

> Name: *Jazz Sethi*
> Current city: *Delhi*
> Favourite quote: *Don't expect things to happen. Struggle and make them happen!*

But the column that brought a broad smile to my face, more than any other information that I might have found, was her relationship status. Single!

After a few minutes of elaborate 'research', I took a moment to assess the situation. She's single, which means I have a chance. I was ready to struggle and was surer of my chances with her after spending some more time analysing her profile. One thing was definite. This wasn't just a random online encounter. I kept wishing that I could record the moment I first saw her for all eternity, not with a camera, but something far, far better. Something that would allow me to know the taste of her lips without mine touching them, something that would enable me to remember her scent and gaze at her ethereal beauty endlessly, something that would eliminate the physical distance between us and make me feel as if we weren't under two different skies, something that could make this fantasy come true and connect me to her. This feeling scared me.

Love never does come easy but there are no equations to prove whether it's really love or just a play of the mind that feigns momentary infatuation. Then there lies the actual problem where one realizes it was love after it's too late. I wanted to make sure that my feelings existed for all the right reasons but I had no way of finding out. I made the executive decision to go slow, deliberating upon ways to share my feelings with her. I didn't have the guts to send her a friend request from my profile; I was too insecure. What if she rejected it instantly? What if she kept it pending for days? What if, like my previous experiences in love, she left me for someone else? Myriad foreboding thoughts raced through my mind, but one of them remained, predominant—I *had to* get to know Jazz.

Thus began my journey on Facebook. Often enough, the important decisions in our lives are governed by our gut. Before I knew it, I had created a fake account on Facebook, under the name Aadi, with a few group photographs but no detailed information about me.

Friend request sent!

Dipika was completely unaware of what I was up to. She would have worn me out with endless lectures on being authentic and true to my real self and whatnot, and I didn't want to deal with any of that right now. Not because she was wrong but because I was insecure about revealing my real self to Jazz. What would she think when she received my friend request? Would she read anything into it? Had I been too forward? What would it mean if she didn't accept it right away? Trivial are the questions that lurk in the minds of over-thinkers and lovers, but they continue to plague them nonetheless. I'm sure even after spending some time together on the balcony, the 2013 version of Romeo would have doubts and apprehensions about his pending friend request to Juliet. In the twenty-first century, a Pakistani citizen waiting to have his visa accepted by the American embassy has it easier than a boy waiting for a girl to accept his friend request on social media.

Delhi

Sipping a cup of coffee and listening to her favourite songs on her iPod, Jazz sat in the balcony enjoying the evening breeze. Her mother kept calling out for her to clean the almirah as it was a weekend, but she wasn't in the mood.

'Not today, Mom. Next week for sure,' she yelled back.

Jazz was not lazy, just preoccupied with trying to come up with an appropriate caption for a selfie she wanted to upload on Facebook. Ignoring the pop-up that momentarily distracted her, she uploaded the photo, checking the caption twice, and then moved on to her notifications. A government employee clears pending files faster than Jazz cleared pending friend requests on her Facebook profile. Although she accepted a few people randomly, it was more a lottery system, mostly depending on her mood. On that day, my luck and Jazz's mood didn't favour me. She saw the pending request from Aadi and rejected it immediately. Why wouldn't she? I was a stranger, after all.

Before going to bed, she went through her nightly ritual of checking her phone, and there was another friend request pending from the same person she had rejected a few hours ago—Aadi. *What kind of a weirdo resends a request that was turned down? On the very same day!* Jazz thought. Pissed off, she rejected the request yet again and turned off her room lights, moving on to the next thing on her schedule.

In another room, elsewhere, another light remained on, as an insecure boy pretending to be someone else, dejected and rejected, desperately hoped to find his salvation. Girls don't know or understand that the hurt caused by virtual rejection is just as painful as being rejected in real life.

Mumbai

She will accept. She won't. She will accept. She won't. I kept refreshing my Facebook app in the hope of receiving an answer I would've liked to see. Gone are the days when a lovesick guy could decide whether a girl was interested by plucking rose petals, where the final petal would indicate his fate. My fate was pending in her notification inbox. Although she had rejected the request once I sent it to her again. After all, she might have done so accidentally. I fervently hoped that she wouldn't see it as desperation, but as eagerness to be friends with her. An hour later, it became harder to remain optimistic. I mean, why would she accept my request? I didn't have Virat Kohli's looks, neither did I have Hrithik Roshan's personality. At least Facebook didn't add salt to my wounds by sending me a rejection notification. Finally, I decided to drop her a message. The only way to catch her attention was to fake it a little more. Genius.

> Hi,
> You sound like a pretty interesting person, which is why I'm sending you this message. You might not be aware of this, but I am Dipika's brother. Dipika Tanna, your friend. Anyway, I'd like to suggest the Twilight series to you; I'm assuming if you liked the movies this much, you'll love the books even more!
> Cheers,
> Aadi
> PS: Do you have a pug? Just my opinion, but I think every girl should have a pug. They are so awesome.

I checked the message again for typos. Satisfied with the absence of grammatical errors after the fourth round of checking, I pressed 'send' and mentally prepared myself for the excruciating wait for her to reply. But to my surprise, Jazz saw the message not too long after I sent it and this sent chills down my spine. I quickly reread the message and shut the chat window as soon as I saw the three dots that indicated that she was typing her reply. A bundle of nerves, I went offline because even though I was desperate, she didn't need to know that.

1 Notification Received

It was her message! Her first message. Fuck, fuck! The feeling that washed over me was comparable to winning a gold medal at the Olympics! Excitedly, I opened the chat box.

Jazz: *Hey, sorry, I wasn't aware of your connection with Dipika. So I ignored the previous request. I'm impressed that you researched me before sending a message. But your research lacked depth. I hate reading, but yes, I do love pugs.*

Goodness gracious! Not bad at all. Slightly off target, but still a decent attempt, I thought. The virtual world is an amazing place to be in if you're looking to brew a new romance, for there is never a lull in conversation; the girl's profile itself provides a long list of conversation starters. If after you go through a girl's profile, you can't think of a question to ask her based on the information there, don't message her at all. But if you can just pick one detail you think is cool, or something that you're genuinely curious about, ask her about it. And, guess what, it works! A short conversation ensued about our general likes and dislikes. Although I knew at the back of my mind that Jazz only accepted my request because she thought I was Dipika's brother, I was okay with it. I was ready to be her father too, but that would have become oddly complicated. I wanted her, I wanted us and I wanted it all with her and only her. I wanted to play with her hair, tell her that I liked her. But was she really interested in taking things forward or had I only been accepted because of a fake connection? At the end of the day, I still didn't know if she was interested.

The next day when I logged into Facebook, I saw that Jazz was online. I paused awkwardly. The person I liked was online but I didn't know what to say even though all I fantasized about was talking to her. But before I could type something carefully thought out and witty, she went offline.

Damn it! I cursed my luck as I refreshed my Messenger to check if there was a network issue. She was still offline. I decided to leave her a message instead.

> *I have so much to tell you, but don't know where to start. I've been through a lot in my life that I can never explain. My heart was shattered a decade ago and I have even come close to believing that love is a sin. I've tried to fix the damage and if I'm being completely honest here, I have to say that love terrified me at one point. But I've realized that every person comes in our life to take us closer to our destiny. They play their role and depart; no one stays with us forever. If something doesn't work out, it doesn't mean one should give up on life. Those days taught me a lot and made me a better*

person, and I am glad that it happened. But there is no point in crying for the rest of your life. So I took the positives and moved on—each person has the right to be happy. Ever since, I have lived with my close friends and family in exhilaration. You might think that I'm making this up. But we were both connected through Facebook. Don't you think it's destiny? I feel that there is a real connection here, even though it was made through a virtual medium. Though I'm not yet sure if it's love, I am sure it's something more than just friendship.

I was about to send her the message when I realized that she was back online. A sudden sensation ran through my nerves and made me numb. My hands began to sweat. I deleted the entire message and sent a 'Hi' in its place, only to curse myself later.

You can never change. You will remain a fat, ugly, brainless soul, I thought angrily.

Jazz: *Hey, what's up?*
Me: *Was just thinking about shifting to Delhi but then decided Mumbai is a better place to live.*

Holy shit! Where did that come from? Delhi? Mumbai? Whaaat?

Jazz: *Delhi is way better, dude. Delhiites rock in every aspect.*

Me: *Do they now? Care to explain?*
Jazz: *See, in Delhi, however severe the summers are—you may sweat buckets and collapse in a puddle—at least you get to experience a change in the seasons. Till it gets really cold. And then you feel like you'll freeze to death. But that's the beauty of it. Everything goes to extremes here. Whereas Mumbai summers—you mean humid with a chance of warm? And winter—you mean humid with a chance of chill?*
Me: *Whatever, at least we don't need to change our work timings or waste space storing voluminous sweaters.*

It's a trap. It's a trap! I shouted in my mind. *Damn, what am I even discussing?* I wondered whether I was a romance writer or a news channel weather reporter.

Jazz: *But Delhi is a meat eater's heaven. Perfect for different appetites and budgets, from street food at Paranthewali Gali and Dilli Haat to Thai, Chinese and Italian at Khan Market and Defence Colony. Also, it has pyaaz and aloo, not kandha and batata like in Mumbai.*
Me: *Though our kandha and batata sounds friendlier, you score in that regard. But don't even get me started on the Mumbai rains. The rains bring out a whole new side of the city; there is a hint of magic, a raw clarity to life that is thrilling, edgy and sublime, all at the same*

time. Mumbai is truly a city of sparkly lights. Sorry, but Delhi has nothing to offer that can match the view of the Arabian Sea or the feel of the breeze as you walk along Juhu beach.

Jazz: *Delhi has a better nightlife and you need to accept that.*

Me: *But you always need to be on guard against the aggressiveness of the people, the nasty cab drivers and the service staff. Mumbai allows you to have fun as and when you want it.*

I desperately need pills or serious relationship advice, because this is starting to look like a disaster! Instead of discussing possible romantic inclinations and interests, we were having a good-for-nothing debate on Delhi versus Mumbai.

Jazz: *Delhi provides you a lot in terms of weekend getaways, from river rafting in Rishikesh to long drives on the Yamuna Expressway to Agra. Delhi doesn't hold you back or disappoint you.*

Me: *Do I need to mention Goa? Everyone wants to go to Goa at least once a year, and you need to live in Mumbai to make that a reality.*

Call it a stroke of luck or destiny or whatever, but this insipid discussion served as the perfect icebreaker. It helped us grow closer and get to know each other better. As the days passed, our conversations became more personal and we exchanged phone numbers. From Facebook to WhatsApp, the journey had thus far been rewarding and enchanting. And since then my taste has changed from pani puri to golgappe.

As I thought about the distance between us, I started to dream about seeing her, being in her presence, even if just for an instant. When I looked at the sky, I thought about time, *How fast will it fly?* I couldn't answer any of the questions that ran through my head—*Why was she so unique? How can she be so complete? So perfect?*

With every passing day, I realized that I could, in fact, fall in love. I was so lost in our conversations that I completely forgot that she had no clue at all about Aditya—she had been talking to Dipika's brother Aadi all this time, something I knew I had to come clean about soon if I didn't want to end up losing her. I hadn't been honest with her about a lot of things. She hated reading, which is why I never told her about the writer in me. I could have kept living a lie but the right thing to do was to tell her the truth. The entire episode was kept hidden from Dipika and although I wanted to confess, I had no way to explain myself. Even Jazz hadn't discussed me with her friends, Randeep and Priyanshi, for neither of us could have anticipated what would happen later.

Lies always have a way of catching up with you.

Can I Borrow Your Companionship 24/7?

'Dad! Why haven't you recharged my Internet plan this month?' Priyanshi inquired over the phone.

'It took you this long enough to figure it out?' her dad asked, his voice dripping with sarcasm.

Priyanshi tried to remain calm and not react but she had to tread carefully from here on.

'You know, I got a message from the website where you're registered for online classes.' He paused for a second and added, 'Do you want to know what it said?'

Please let it be something good, please.

'They mentioned that you haven't been attending the classes for a long time now and since you shouldn't lag behind, I requested them to make the recordings of those classes available to you. But what has been going on?'

Her whole body was trembling in apprehension of what was to come next. *Be brave*, her brain cheered but she was too consumed with fear. When she didn't reply, her father continued speaking.

'It seems you've made some great friends on Facebook. So you might need an Internet pack for the same, right?' The sarcasm and contempt was really hard to miss now.

Priyanshi froze. She felt the tears threatening to spill at any moment. She didn't want to cry. She didn't want to seem weak in front of her dad.

Finding her voice, she replied, 'I was just focusing on other subjects . . . that's why I missed a few classes.' She tried to explain but . . .

'We all know how important it is for you to clear your UPSC exam, otherwise you'll just be a disgrace. Although I must say you are proving to be quite a disappointment already. I personally don't like your interest in the civil services. Though it's a complete waste of time, we have invested a lot in you now. Don't let us down.' With those wonderful words of wisdom, Priyanshi's father cut the call.

What do you like? You love reputation and money. But I don't. If I want to join the civil services, I will. If only I were that brave and determined. A tear fell down on her cheek.

Everything Priyanshi did had to be perfect, from her grades to the way she organized her room. Of course, her brother always got a free pass because he could do no wrong. Back in his college days, if he failed, there was just a mild 'Try harder next time', but if she had committed a similar offence, she would've been greeted with a 'Stay in your room with no technology until you know the textbook backwards and forwards'. She remembered an incident where her brother took novels from her shelf and, before she could even grasp what was going on, tore them to shreds and threw them in the dustbin, telling her that he controlled her future and ordering her to never disobey him. Her family's influence had followed her to Delhi. The pressure was too much to handle. It was not as if she didn't study, but she needed mental peace as well. It was only because of Randeep and Jazz and their friendship that she had managed to make a few good memories.

Regardless of what she feels, I need to tell her everything today. It's already gone on for too long; it's now or never. Even if she gets angry with me and abuses me, I'll be calm and composed. I sat directly across from Dipika, thoughts of confessing, and the aftermath, tormenting me.

'I have something I need to apologize to you for, Dipika,' I began.

'Really? And what's that?' She looked confused.

I really hope that she doesn't kill me after hearing this. Go ahead, Aditya, speak up.

'I pretended to be your brother to talk to a girl.'

Okay, kill me. She didn't look angry, but shocked.

'Where was the need for that, dude?' She pretended to stay cool. Her calmness was disconcerting.

'You were the only person we had in common. I wanted to tell you before but it never seemed like the right time. I didn't have the guts,' I confessed.

'Why are you confessing now?'

'Because we have planned to meet and I want you to come along. She thinks I am your brother and is completely unaware of my true identity.'

I knew of the tough times that lay ahead of me and even though it was a little too much to ask of her, I wanted Dipika to be by my side, like a true friend.

'Who is the girl?'

'Jazz. Priyanshi's friend.'

Should I have brought a gun for her to shoot me with, or would she prefer to kill me painfully and slowly? I thought to myself.

Finally, after narrating the whole story to her, I felt like my chest was a few kilograms lighter. Dipika was furious though.

'Are you fucking crazy? Do you even realize the consequences of what you've done?' She continued, 'She may never have heard about you before or seen you, but Priyanshi knows you well.'

'So what are you saying?'

'The point is that Priyanshi knows you and I wonder how she hasn't realized it yet. You should be scared and ashamed. I advise you to reveal your real identity before taking a step further. You're giving someone false expectations. It will definitely backfire.'

'So in simple words, I've fucked my own ass. What should I do now?'

'All you can do is hope that no one reveals the truth to her before you come clean. You know girls hate lies and liars.' She shot me a meaningful look while I just sat there speechless, looking guilty, wondering how I could have been so stupid.

Dipika was my closest friend and she was right. Her reaction made me realize that the situation was worse than I had imagined. Instead of soothing me like a citrusy lemonade that rids you of a terrible hangover, Dipika was the lemon that was squeezed on open wounds to exacerbate the pain. I thought about what my first encounter with Jazz would be like. I played multiple scenarios in my head in which I told her the truth and then anticipated her reaction. Not a single one worked in my favour. Each ended disastrously, like a car accident you know is going to happen, but can do nothing to stop. I was devastated and wondered if crying myself to sleep might make things a little more bearable. The possible fallout of telling Jazz the truth haunted me all day and thoughts of her leaving me followed me to bed that night.

Priyanshi was still frustrated after the conversation with her father and was redirecting her anger at her pillow. As she struggled to move under the heavy layers of blankets, trying to get them off her, she kicked and pushed, her hands reaching out into empty space, all in vain. Her legs gave up. Just then, she heard the sound of the knob turning and turned to see the door open and Jazz rush in. She wanted to tell Priyanshi about meeting Dipika's brother Aadi for the first time, but with one look at Priyanshi's face, she knew something was wrong.

'Are you okay? You look sick.'

'It's nothing serious,' Priyanshi replied, almost too quickly. Hoping Jazz hadn't noticed, she continued, 'What brings you here?'

'Are you okay?' Now there was a question that perhaps no one ever, in the history of the world, answered truthfully. Most people prefer to plaster on a smile and pretend everything is normal. Priyanshi was no different.

She faked a smile to reassure Jazz, hoping her friend would see through the façade and see how she wasn't okay, how she hadn't been okay for a very long time. But Jazz was preoccupied with her own reasons for coming to see Priyanshi.

'I am meeting your friend's brother,' Jazz announced. 'I don't know how to say this, but I kind of like him. He seems like a decent guy,' she added, blushing.

This caught Priyanshi's attention 'Which friend?'

'Dipika.'

'Dipika has a brother? She never told me. How do you know him?'

Jazz hesitated a little before answering. 'We met on Facebook. We have been chatting with each other for some time now. He's coming to Delhi for work and casually suggested that we meet. I casually agreed.'

She began telling Priyanshi about how she met Aadi, from the very beginning, and then showed the photos she had. The second she saw the photographs, Priyanshi figured out the truth.

'This is Aditya, Dipika's *friend*, who's a writer. He is definitely not her brother.'

'What?' Jazz exclaimed in shock.

'Yes, I'm damn sure. She's told me about him several times before. He's her good friend. I'm sure there's been a misunderstanding.'

'No. In fact, I understand perfectly now.' Jazz didn't wait for Priyanshi to answer. She just got up and left, taking her bag and betrayal with her. She would call Priyanshi later and explain, she'd understand. Jazz just needed to be alone right then. Walking further away from Priyanshi's apartment, she went to a park and sat on a bench, recollecting how it had all started and how it hadn't even taken a minute for it to shatter right before her. She doubted everything he had said to her. It had all been a lie. She felt a crushing weight engulf her. She couldn't focus on anything any more. Her senses that had been so alive these past few weeks were now numb, having realized that it had all been just an illusion. None of it was true.

She thought about calling him and asking for an explanation, but she decided to clear things up in person instead. She messaged Priyanshi asking her not to reveal what she knew to Dipika or anyone else for that matter. She eagerly waited for the moment when she could demand an explanation. Her previous excitement had transformed into anger, her curiosity replaced with betrayal and her faith changed into disgust.

She thought to herself, *A snake you were. Stalking me using my profile, you devised your plan to kill everything inside me. Skilfully you weaved your web, planted your trap. And all this while I believed you. I let your words blindfold me. I'm game now. My trust, your weapon. You deceived, I believed. You want to play me, right? Now you'll be sorry you crossed paths with me.*

'This is the final announcement for all passengers travelling to Delhi via Jet Airways.'

'You're nervous. Here, have a drink, it'll calm you down.'

Turning down the Coke that Dipika was offering me, I couldn't help but feel a little irritated with her. She had badgered me with her advice and her lectures throughout our ride to the airport. But then again, she hadn't judged me once. More importantly, setting aside her priorities in Mumbai, she accompanied me to Delhi. Now that's a true friend!

'Let's board. Have you informed her that you're coming?' She was referring to Jazz. 'I think you should ask her to pick us up from the airport.'

If only she would remain quiet and let me think for some time! *Can you please, just please, not talk for the next few minutes, Dipika?* I envisioned duct tape covering her mouth, but I knew I couldn't be mad at her.

I was finally going to meet the girl of my dreams, the one who had successfully swept me off my feet. It all seemed unreal to me, ethereal almost, like a dream, but I knew this was all really happening. I was ecstatic, but at the back of my mind, I was scared too. And nervous. It was time for me to confess the truth to her. Stolen glances, half-uttered words dying away, letting the awkward silence win—that's what first dates are all about, right? However, my encounter could hardly be called a date. In fact, I felt like I was going to the confession box to divulge my sins.

I shouldn't have lied at the beginning. Nothing comes easy but why complicate things further with lies? I did lie though, and now I have to live through the horror.

My feelings for her couldn't be called love just yet, but they were almost there. It definitely wasn't just about lust for me. I knew that I wasn't in love yet, but my feelings for her were strong and true.

Once we landed, I sent Jazz a message.

Me: *Landed. Waiting for the evening. Lots to catch up on.*
Jazz: *Indeed. Welcome. Delhi has a lot to offer. See you at the Saket mall in the evening.*
Me: *I'm sure the wait will be worth it.*

After checking into the hotel, Dipika relaxed in the room while I started the day. All my thoughts, since I had left Mumbai, had been about Jazz. We'd been talking these past few days and judging from our conversations, I could tell that she liked talking to me. But this meeting could change everything forever. I was the same person, just with a different name. Everything that I had said to her had been the truth, my intentions had been pure. I was just insecure about rejection, but would she understand that? More importantly, even if she did, would she trust me again?

Forget the risk, and take the fall. If it's meant to be, then it's worth it all. Sometimes overthinking kills our ability to be happy. We have no control over our heart. There is no logic to loving someone. You connect with someone instantly and that's it.

Feeling down, alone and empty on the inside, Jazz was still hurting from pain caused by the duplicity of the person she had trusted. Lost in her thoughts, she drifted off into the comforting embrace that unconsciousness had to offer.

He drifts in, like the gentleness of a stream.
It all happens so fast!
Wake up . . . it's not a dream.
Before you know
You're giving and he's taking
But you are blind to this deception,
As he uses his insecurities as a weapon.

He needs your love, he says.
But you also have needs of your own!
You're falling, he begs for your forgiveness . . .
And you go back . . . only to be hurt again.
Wake up . . . it's not a dream!

Her alarm jerked her back to the real world. The clock indicated that she was nearer to the moment of truth, and as she started getting dressed, she thought about how she would soon undress the layers of lies and hear the naked truth.

Both Jazz and I were anxious about our first encounter but for different reasons. While I waited to confess, she waited to express; I wanted to start a new chapter, she wanted to edit the last one. While I wanted to show love, she wanted to blow up in anger. While I believed she was clueless about the truth, she knew more than she would have liked to know.

'I am Aditya, not Aadi. I lied. I wanted to talk to you without letting you know my identity because I was scared and nervous. I wanted to talk to you as a genuine person, someone whom you would like to talk to. Although in reality, I *am* genuine. Genuinely genuine. Please forgive me. My feelings for you are extremely genuine.' I rehearsed my confession in front of Dipika, sitting at a café in the mall.

'If you repeat your monologue once more, Aditya, trust me, dude, I will kick your ass. *Genuinely.* This is the zillionth time I've heard the same bullshit.' Dipika looked pissed off.

'You don't understand what I am going through,' I explained, hoping to get through to her. She responded with a glare.

Calm down, Aditya, you have got to be in control. And stop drinking water for God's sake. You're already eight glasses down, my brain yelled, but I drank the ninth glass of water anyway. And soon I needed to use the loo.

What if she enters the café at the same moment? Maybe I should hold it in and go later. But what if I piss my pants while confessing the truth? I'd better go now.

As luck would have it, just as I was about to unzip my pants, my phone rang. Without even looking at the caller ID, I knew it was her. Cursing my luck, I picked up her call anyway.

'Hey, have you reached?' I threw a question at her before she could say anything.

'Yes, I'm at the café. Where exactly are you?'

I'm in the loo, peeing! I wish I could just die already.

'Err . . . near the counter. Give me a minute?' I finished my business quickly and went outside.

My eyes wandered all over the place, trying to recognize her familiar face in an unfamiliar crowd. I finally saw her as she turned to face me, talking on the phone with someone, completely oblivious to my presence, unaware that my eyes were trying to take in every aspect of her. She was drop-dead gorgeous! Dressed in a denim jumpsuit and sneakers, she was a traffic stopper who could hypnotize anyone who came her way. She stood alone and, even from a distance, I could tell she was perfect; I was looking at the most beautiful girl I'd ever laid eyes on. It was an unfamiliar feeling. No, not lust, but perhaps it was love that took over my senses in that moment. Never would I have imagined that love would strike me at first sight, but all that changed when I saw her. That's when I realized she was looking at me too.

'Hey, Aadi,' she said, coming over to where I was standing.

'Jazz.' I barely managed to get her name out.

'Come, let's take a seat.'

I led her towards the table where I'd left Dipika earlier; they exchanged pleasantries.

'Dipika, you're his sister, right?' Maybe I was imagining it but in that moment I was certain there was an edge to Jazz's voice when she asked that question.

'Umm . . .' Hesitantly, I changed the topic, hoping she wouldn't notice. 'Sorry you had to wait.'

When I heard her voice, a new world had opened up to me. A sound so gorgeous flowed from her lips that it threw me into a tizzy. Dipika pinched me hard under the table and brought me back to reality. It was time to tell her that Dipika was not my sister.

'I wanted to tell you something. Just hear me out first before you say anything?'

'I wanted to say something as well . . .'

'Oh? You should go first then.' I smiled.

That gives me another few minutes. I hope what she has to say lasts for hours. Or a lifetime maybe.

She paused for a few short seconds before saying the last thing I expected.

'I have come to a conclusion. You are just a typical guy who is here for one thing. Unless you can prove to me that you want more, I have no intentions of associating myself with the pain, the lying, the feeling of being dejected, the anger and hate that you've put me through.' Seeing my shocked expression, by a way of explanation, she continued, 'Yes, that's right. I know everything. Didn't you feel even the slightest bit of guilt before lying to me? Or is your entire life built on a foundation of lies?'

She didn't wait for me to respond. 'Look, Priyanshi told me everything. Fortunately for me, when I told her about you, she didn't even think twice before revealing the truth, and unfortunately for you, I am ending this right here.'

Jazz started to get up to leave but Dipika made her sit down again, pleading with her to listen to the entire truth before she left.

I took a deep breath and began. 'I was here to confess the same thing to you, but I see that you're familiar with the truth anyway. Yes, I used a fake ID but I didn't use fake photographs or a fake phone number. Even though the name I used was different, I'm the same guy you've been talking to all these weeks. You wouldn't have given me a chance had I not lied. I know you're hurt. I don't know what I was thinking. But I just wanted to get to know you, and for you to get to know me. I didn't think you'd find out the truth on your own. You had said that you didn't like to read, so it was highly unlikely that you would have come across any of my books. I wanted you to talk to me as a regular person. I liked you and I approached you for all the right reasons. My intentions never have been, and never will be, wrong. As our conversations grew longer, I realized you were more wonderful as a person than I first thought you to be. I got to know a girl who is excited about the small things, who lives for her passions and holds things close to her heart, and such a girl, in my opinion, is worth knowing, and worth every risk.'

I looked at Jazz eagerly, but she replied coldly, 'You lied and I hate liars. Please don't ask me to meet you again.'

She left and there was nothing that either Dipika or I could say to stop her. Even in my wildest dreams, I couldn't have envisioned it all unfolding like this. I hadn't expected this connection to end so soon, and so abruptly. It felt like even before our book of love could take off, the author had writer's block.

The moment she left is the moment that I realized that everything is subject to change. Expecting constancy and sameness is equivalent to playing with fire and not expecting to get hurt. If there was anyone I held responsible for the way things had turned out between us, it was me. Somehow, I have a knack for screwing up every single thing I touch. The pain of rejection had begun to build up inside me and I was in need of catharsis . . . but what I needed most desperately was her. Although Dipika advised me to stay calm and not make any hasty moves, I decided to text Jazz.

Please come back, don't end it like this. There was more to it. Certainly! I swear my objective was not to hurt you. Though my acts have left bruises on your heart, I am still the same person. The one you talked with at length, defending your city's magnificence all through the night. It is only for you that I post anything on Facebook, in the hopes of receiving a comment. You cannot deny that we do have something special. Please don't end it like this. At least give it a chance.

Her reply came sooner than I expected.

Enough is enough. I'm sure that what you're saying now is also part of some cock-and-bull story, an elaborate plan to get all the benefits while you still can. I'm a simple person and I value relationships. I'm sensitive of the small things in life, and that is exactly why I cannot bear to stand having my heart broken any further. I'll have nothing left then. I'll be devoid of emotions, sanity and trust. After what you did, I don't think I can trust you any more. All I expected you to do was man up and tell me the truth.

It was one of those moments when you realize that no matter what you do, no matter what you say, the end is near. I fervently wished that I had had more conversations with her in real life than in my head. Really, sometimes I wish I hadn't even got involved. I should've just left it at hello and gone with the flow.

July 2015
Bandra

'What happened next? Why have you stopped? Please continue.' Roma seemed irritated as we paused our story to order another round of drinks.

'I thought we could repeat our drinks,' I answered.

'I don't need another drink. I need more details. Why didn't you send her a request as your real self, Aditya?'

'I suppose I was scared as I am not a person who can flirt openly. I'm a little reserved, you can say. Also, if she had known that I was a writer, her perception towards me would have changed. Moreover, it wasn't really a fake profile. It was another profile meant only for my close friends. So I thought of adding Jazz to it. After all, I wanted to know her closely. So I didn't lie as such but portrayed the partial truth. If she had rejected me upfront, I had an alternative.'

Jazz smiled as she looked around for the waiter.

'I wanted to order a chicken . . .' She paused and turned towards me. 'What's that chicken you get here?'

'Umm . . .'

'Chicken sixty-nine. Make that one.'

'Sixty-nine? Ma'am, we don't have such a dish,' the waiter apologized.

'I have ordered it many times. Ask your manager.'

'Do you mean chicken sixty-five?' I was confused.

'Oh fuck, yeah . . . One chicken sixty-five.'

We all burst out laughing.

'How did you feel when you found out he had lied to you?' Roma was like a dog with a bone.

'Don't ask! I wanted to . . . make chicken sixty-five out of him.'

'Go ahead then, tell us. Even I want to know.' I leaned forward, looking at her.

'I was so pissed that I wanted to set his hair on fire. I wanted to use every cuss word I knew and scream it at him. But Priyanshi was the voice of reason and told me that even though he had used a fake ID to talk to me, he hadn't misused any information or crossed any lines while chatting. Rather, he had been very decent. It was because of her that I agreed to step out of my house and have a word with Aditya that day. Otherwise I was all set to block him. In fact, after the last message I sent him, I did block him,' Jazz explained.

Often, we find ourselves with things that need to be said, but no words to express them, when we need to understand the situation but are too blinded by anger. At our lowest times, during our toughest moments, life seems to get complicated and confusing, leaving us wondering what the other person is thinking or feeling. Often, we let pride get in the way and we lose the power and sense to communicate. But I believed in Jazz and our relationship and all that we had shared in that short span of time. I believed that we'd get through it. I knew she was hiding behind her anger and had the truth locked away. There is often so much said even in the things that we don't say. Even so, I owed the success of our relationship to Priyanshi, who gave me a chance without even knowing me!

'So where *is* Priyanshi these days? And Randeep?' Roma asked.

'Randeep is abroad, he's enjoying his life. And . . .' I looked at Jazz who didn't react.

Dipika interrupted me by alerting us to the approaching waiter.

'Your chicken sixty-nine is here,' I teased.

'Shut up.' Jazz kicked me under the table.

'This is what happens when you watch too many sex comedies. Not that I have a problem with that, you know.' I winked.

Jazz ignored me and took a bite of the chicken, and Roma's interrogation continued.

'So how did you convince Jazz?'

'He was fortunate enough that Priyanshi was a close friend of mine. She was very supportive once I convinced her that Aditya never had any evil intentions.' Dipika smiled.

'It was not easy. It never is,' I added. There are no fixed rules to mend a broken heart; different people react to a broken heart differently. Convincing her was no less than cracking the IIT and IIM entrance exams.

In Search of Vitamin 'Love'

The Earth had rotated twice about its axis, people on my friends list had already changed their WhatsApp display pictures at least five times, Dipika had finished watching an entire season of *Friends* once again and I was still waiting in the capital city of India, exactly where I had been two days ago, waiting for her to unblock me. Such is life.

'Will this endless waiting ever end? It's starting to suffocate me now. Isn't she being a little too dramatic?' I asked the two girls sitting in front of me. I was at a café with Priyanshi and Dipika. Like the girl I was desperately hoping to talk to, these two had decided to ignore me as well. Great!

While Priyanshi tapped her feet to the music, Dipika furiously tapped away on her phone. I checked WhatsApp for the umpteenth time.

Girls will never change. They just want to establish their authority over men. I am stuck between three of them. Hello, can you hear me?

Finally, Priyanshi took pity on me and broke the silence. 'She is a girl, Aditya,' she said before getting lost in the music again.

Oh, really now? I didn't know that. For two whole days, here I've been, waiting in Delhi, sitting with her friend, just to hear that the person I love is a girl! Wow! That's some news.

'Is this going to last forever or will it end some day? I mean all she has to do is unblock me and give me a chance to at least explain myself!' I'd never been this frustrated.

'Dude, blocking someone is not a game for us. We use it as a weapon to harass the one we love.'

Wait, did she say 'love'? Love? Jazz doesn't love me, from what she told me two days ago, I think she hates me! Someone has to decode the workings of a girl's mind and explain them to me! And while they're at it, maybe they should reprogram their minds to stop blocking people for little things. I mean, who does that? Girls, who else!

'I'm serious,' I said to them.

'Okay. Let's get back to work,' Priyanshi said.

'Aditya, don't you get it? Jazz is a girl. More importantly, she is currently an *angry* girl. You need to spoil her a little bit.' Dipika patted my back.

'Spoil?'

'Yes, you need to make her feel special,' Priyanshi explained. *Finally we're getting somewhere!*

'How do I do that?'

'You mean before WhatsApp, people didn't pamper anyone? Huh?'

'Umm . . . let me think.'

Priyanshi was about to say something when her phone fell to the ground. As she bent down to pick it up, one of the café employees brushed against her on purpose. Immediately Priyanshi reacted and tried to catch hold of him as he started walking away as if nothing had happened.

Turning around, he violently shook off her arm and started screaming racial comments.

'You Nepali chinki, don't touch me. Go back to your country!'

Before he could say anything else, I punched him hard on the nose. I couldn't just let him get away with it. A few punches later, the café manager separated us. If he hadn't interrupted us, I might have left the guy unconscious.

'How can you hire such racist employees?' Turning towards the employee who was clutching his bloody nose, I roared, 'You think she is from some other country? She is an Indian citizen, from the North-east. We belong to the same country, for God's sake! And even if she was some foreigner in your café, what gives you the right to touch

50

her? Fucking moron. I will file a complaint against you and your café. You think you'll get away with it and joke about it later? You should meet me outside and, trust me, it will be the last thing you ever do!'

I offered Priyanshi some water and sat next to her as she looked shaken up. Dipika took the seat in front of her.

'Are you okay?' Dipika inquired.

'Yeah. I'm fine. This is nothing new.'

'You should never let these bastards get away.' I took the water bottle from her hand and placed it on the table.

The café manager didn't charge us for our coffee but Dipika insisted that we pay, so I obliged. As we walked out of the café, I held Priyanshi's arm to calm her down but released her immediately, thinking she might not like it.

'Thanks for standing up for me. You aren't that bad a guy. Jazz is very lucky.' That's all she said before taking off.

It did hurt, that was certain. The more she ignored me, the more I was drawn to her. Love is a strange feeling indeed. I wanted to hate her and forget all about her; I wanted to move on. I couldn't deal with her tantrums. But the more I thought about it, the more I realized that my heart would always get in the way. I was in a constant battle with myself, and love was certainly winning over hate.

I woke up in the middle of the night thinking I was all alone in this world, a world full of people who never seemed to care. I tried recalling the last time I had had a good night's sleep, but couldn't, so I put on some very loud music to drown out my thoughts. I couldn't hear anything but the sound of my heart beating, thumping to the rhythm of the music. And that's when I found a way out of the mess. I recalled being handed a pamphlet by someone at the café before the incident with Priyanshi took place. Quickly, I checked my pockets to locate it.

Arijit Singh and a Grand Symphony of 60 Musicians.
Live in concert at Leisure Valley, Gurgaon.

I remembered from Jazz's Facebook profile that she was a huge fan of Arijit's music. This was the sign I'd been waiting for! I called the numbers printed on the pamphlet to inquire about tickets, but there was no answer. I checked my clock—3 a.m.

Too late to call. Maybe I should ask Priyanshi if this would work.

'Hi. I'm sorry to disturb you so late at night. But it's urgent. Can you talk?'

'Now that you have already called, continue.' She sounded like she was half asleep.

'There is a concert. Arijit Singh, live in Gurgaon. Do you think it will work?'

'Yes, yes. She is a big fan. Perhaps it's a sign that your time has come,' she said in a firm voice.

'Okay then, I'm booking our tickets. Should I book one for Randeep too?'

'Umm . . . No. He'll be at his friend's party. Saturday nights are precious and rare.' She laughed.

The first thing I did next morning was to call and ask if there were tickets available. Fortunately, there were, and without further thought, I bought them. Then I asked Dipika to drop Jazz a message and to call Priyanshi and inform her. After a few hours, I got a message from Priyanshi.

Priyanshi: *Yes, she is coming. She has agreed because it's Arijit Singh.*
Me: *What! Fuck, are you serious?*
Priyanshi: *Yes, but only for Arijit. Not you . . .*
Me: *Arijit or Aditya, I don't care. What matters is that she's coming. Please handle the rest. I owe you big time!*
Priyanshi: *Calm down, don't get too hyper.*
Me: *I just hope everything goes well.*
Priyanshi: *I hope so too. See you!*

All your senses are sharpened when true love is around the corner, waiting just for you. One glance is enough to blow you away. The sound of her voice calling my name sent shivers through my body, causing my heart to beat faster as a silly grin crept across my face. Inspiration struck me and I fired up my laptop to write, waiting impatiently for evening to approach.

There is just something about those eyes,
It feels like life has pressed pause.
I hope it's not a sin to think about you all day long,
And to see you in my dreams,
To feel your arms around me, protecting me.
There is nowhere I would rather be
Than right here with you beside me.
There is just something about the way you speak
That makes me believe I'll be fine.
I wish you weren't so far away,
I wish I could somehow gather the courage
To look at you and tell you,
I am falling for you.

To say I was hyperventilating when Priyanshi didn't answer my fourth call was an understatement.

'Where are they? Did you call them? Priyanshi is not responding.' I was panicking.

'She must be driving. I've called and confirmed twice with her that they're coming. Should I place a spy camera around her too? Jeez, Aditya!' Dipika said furiously.

I didn't react, but my nerves and the seriousness of the situation were killing me. When I finally saw Priyanshi walking towards us, I thought I'd faint. But when I looked around, searching for Jazz, and didn't see her, I thought I'd die.

'Before you say anything, hear me out! Jazz said she's coming directly to the concert. I'm sure you aren't very excited to see me here alone, but as of now you have no other choice but to wait.' Priyanshi winked.

'Nah . . . it's not like that. I am . . . happy.' I couldn't even convince myself, and Priyanshi clearly saw through my act.

'I can see that.'

Happy? How can I be happy? I am irritated beyond comprehension. Is Jazz really going to come or are these two playing a prank? Should I call her from one of their cell phones, or will she think that's pathetic? I came all this way just to see her, talk to her and express what I feel, to the extent that I'm attending a concert that I couldn't care less about.

Fifteen minutes later, I was beyond impatient. 'The concert is about to start. Please ask her where she is?' I sounded helpless. I was beginning to lose my mind. After all, I was no saint!

'She is not picking up my call. I have already tried and I've left her several messages as well. There's no reply.' Priyanshi looked embarrassed. She was upset about it too.

The concert had begun, and as it progressed, it dawned on me that Jazz wasn't going to turn up at all. Arijit Singh's voice added to my grief. The songs he chose perfectly matched my mood. It was the feeling you got when you started growing apart from a friend, when a movie sucked compared to the book, when you failed a test you studied hard for or when you were hungry and expectantly looked in the fridge only to find no food. Disappointment weighed down on me like an anchor. When you fervently hope for something to bring meaning to your life and make you feel alive, you'll realize that disappointment comes hand in hand. Both Priyanshi and Dipika could see the dejection in my eyes. They tried to cheer me up all through the concert, but nothing could change the way I felt.

After some time, Priyanshi's face lit up. 'I know what you can do, Aditya! Tomorrow, Randeep and Jazz will go zip-lining. I've told him about you. You should join them there; I'll even accompany you.'

'What if she doesn't turn up there as well once she finds out that I'm coming?'

'We won't tell her. It's their routine on weekends, so there's no reason for her to skip it.'

'Yes, yes! This sounds good!' Dipika said excitedly.

I, on the other hand, had mixed up feelings about this plan. I was confused about why I wanted to see her—whether it was my feelings for her, or whether I just wanted an explanation for being rejected by her. I felt like a rudderless ship being tossed about in every direction. But the thought of seeing her once again gave me hope. Maybe this time, I could finally sail ashore.

'Why do you bother challenging me when you know you're going to lose?' Jazz asked Randeep as she set herself up for another zip-line adventure at Flying Fox, Neemrana.

'We need to talk first, Jazz,' Randeep said, his tone businesslike.

Ignoring him, Jazz continued teasing. 'Talk? Are you giving up before the game even starts?'

'Priyanshi is about to reach any minute now and—'

Jazz interrupted him. 'Great! So there are more people coming to see you lose?'

'Ha, ha,' he said, sarcastically. He took a deep breath before continuing, 'I actually I wanted to tell you before but . . .'

'Speak up, Randeep. Don't act like a shy TV serial *bahu*.'

'Aditya is coming along with her,' Randeep blurted out.

'Are you serious? Why? You know everything that happened, so how could you allow it?' Jazz yelled.

'I think you are being a little rude, Jazz. He's a good guy. Priyanshi told me last night about what happened at the café.' Randeep explained patiently, hoping to convince her, but anyone who's ever tried this knows there's no convincing Jazz of anything.

'Are you his lawyer or my friend?' Jazz asked angrily.

Overhearing her last statement as I was entering, I contemplated turning back—I half expected her to throw me from the hilltop when she saw me.

'Here they are.' Randeep pointed towards us.

Too late to run now, I thought.

Jazz looked furious. Though she didn't say a word, her expression spoke volumes. She looked like she could kill me, but there was still a softness in her eyes when she looked at me. Maybe I wasn't completely out of luck. Maybe, just maybe, in some corner of her heart, she had feelings for me too. No matter how hard you try to hide your real feelings, your body language always gives you away.

And then in my sincerest voice, I spoke to her. 'I am really, really sorry, Jazz. Forgive me for my stupidity, please? I'll never lie to you again about anything. I really mean it. Let's be friends at least?' I offered her my hand.

'Really?' she asked suspiciously.

'I promise.'

'Then take this challenge. Randeep takes the same every Sunday,' Jazz said with complete confidence, for she knew she could beat me. My expression must have given me away as I had no idea what she was talking about, because she pointed towards her zip-line kit.

'You mean a zip-line race?' I pretended not to understand her.

'What's wrong? Are you acrophobic?' she challenged.

'I'm up for anything,' I said, feigning confidence.

Aditya, you're a man. Men aren't scared of anything, so you can't be scared at all. Wait! Men can't be scared? Fuck gender roles! Damn, I hate her. But I love her more. I sighed.

She secured herself to the harness while the instructor guided me through the rules. I listened to them very carefully because this was not how I wanted to end my life. As I looked down the line, I silently prayed for my life. I even promised to visit the Siddhivinayak temple once I reached Mumbai safely. I took a look at Jazz; she couldn't have looked more prepared, whereas I felt like I was about to wet my pants.

One second my feet were firmly planted on the ground, the next they were not.

I'm picking up speed. Oh hell. I am dying. This is suicide. Murder. Whatever. I'm dying. Oh lord, oh lord, oh lord! Argh!

I have no control. Mom, Dad, I love you. I love myself too. I don't want to die. Someone get me out of here.

Jazz drifted swiftly whereas I was struggling in the middle of nowhere. I wanted to shout my heart out but hung on helplessly. Jazz started laughing from the end of the line when she saw the instructor helping me out. She had won! I had lost. But at least I had won her friendship, right? That was the prize I'd been after anyway. She was still laughing when I finally reached the finish point.

Once we had all freshened up, we went out for brunch, and although Jazz was as stubborn as a mule and refused to come along, Randeep and Priyanshi played their roles to perfection and convinced her. They made her understand that they wouldn't have suggested meeting me at all if I were a threat to her and that it wouldn't harm her to give friendship a chance, just so she could find out what lay ahead. After considerable effort, she finally gave in. It worked! I had finally found my way in, even if it was just as her friend. I had no choice but to be happy. Trying to understand girls is truly a back-breaking task!

'So will you unblock me so we can start over?'

'Excuse me?'

'I mean . . . are we friends?'

Before she could speak, Randeep interrupted, 'Aditya, let's meet in the evening. I have a fantastic plan for the night!' And he briefed us about it. Everyone agreed and one thing was clear—this guy did not live a normal life. He was always on the lookout for a thrill.

But I wasn't going to let Randeep take away my moment. I offered my hand to Jazz for the second time that day and said, 'Jazz hasn't replied to my question. I'll join you guys if she answers in the affirmative.'

'What question?' Randeep and Priyanshi asked in unison.

I repeated, 'Are we friends?'

'Sure, and I'm sorry.' Jazz smiled and shook my hand. 'Ooohs' and 'aaahs' followed from the other two.

Mission accomplished! Her smile and the touch of her hand made me fall for her all over again. All the transgressions of the past were forgotten; I was looking forward to a bright, hopeful future with Jazz now. Maybe she had just pretended to hate me all these days. Things always find a way to correct themselves with time; all we've got to do is wait.

Ten minutes later . . .

Facebook Notification Received: Jazz has accepted your friend request.

Out of Coverage Area

'I have seen your mail, Ms Tanna. Your synopsis and sample chapters are indeed interesting. But the title needs work. It needs to be something interesting in order to catch the readers' attention,' Mr Roy suggested, taking a sip of his coffee. In his early fifties, Mr Roy ran an independent publishing house and worked actively with his authors. He had an innate ability to understand the pulse of the reading audience and picked up scripts which guaranteed him success. Over a decade, he had delivered many bestselling authors who had changed the face of the industry.

Sitting across him in his plush office, Dipika contemplated his suggestions before answering. 'I'm open to making changes, Mr Roy, but the condition you mentioned in the email worries me.' Resting her hands on the table, she noticed how Roy's bald patch reflected the sunlight coming in through the window.

'That's just the need of the market. Spice it up,' he said, lighting a cigarette.

'No, sir. Coffee and cigarettes needn't complement each other always.'

'But somehow, it tastes better. The final product,' he said, smiling at her slyly.

Dipika hadn't told anyone that she was going to meet a publisher that afternoon. This meeting was another reason for her to be in Delhi, but she wanted to keep it a secret from everyone. The publisher was considering her manuscript, but hadn't yet signed her on. It would have been published by now had Mr Roy not suggested some unnecessary changes just to make her a commercial success, changes that she disagreed with.

Should I consult Aditya about these terms or should I just accept now? I think I should accept and surprise Aditya, she thought.

'Okay, Mr Roy. Give me a couple of weeks to send you a revised manuscript.'

'Please send me your marketing plan so that we can decide on how many copies should be printed in the first run,' Mr Roy added.

'Do I need to pay anything for the same? I've heard that publishers sometimes charge the author for marketing costs. By the way, Aditya is my good friend of mine.'

For a moment, Mr Roy looked shaken until he regained his composure and replied, 'We are a small publishing company, Ms Tanna, but we do not charge our authors. It's your hard work and we should pay for it. I am against authors paying for their own work being published. We believe in following traditional publishing etiquette.'

'Thank you.' She nodded.

After discussing the publishing schedule a little further, Dipika left the office and called Priyanshi to confirm where they were meeting that evening.

'Does Aditya know where to go as well?' she inquired.

'Yes, but I suppose he is waiting for you. Where are you?' asked Priyanshi.

'I am on my way back. I'll call him and see you in few hours.' Dipika hung up.

Fuck, I'm so excited about telling Aditya all about the meeting but I'll wait to surprise him till everything is confirmed and in action. Maybe I'll surprise him with a copy of my book.

Dipika had always been shy about sharing her work with others, so much so that she rarely even updated her status on Facebook. Now she was ready to take a step ahead. She had come to Delhi with only her manuscript, but she was returning to Mumbai with new dreams, hopes and determination.

'So Aditya, are you all geared up for this journey?' Priyanshi asked as she rested her hands on Jazz's shoulders.

'The journey of love or the bicycle journey that we've got planned for today?' I winked.

'Both of them are equally challenging, for sure.'

'As of now, I'm focusing on the latter,' I answered sincerely. We were waiting for Randeep to arrive.

'Sorry, I'm a little late. Delhi traffic sucks,' he said when he finally joined us.

'Mumbai traffic is worse,' I said, sneaking a look at Jazz, who was smiling.

After a light-hearted debate on traffic, we headed towards Stonehead Bikers to rent our bicycles. Randeep had planned a bicycle trip to Camp Tikkling, which was twenty kilometres away. We rented Ryders Act 110 cycles along with the accessories we needed—helmets, water bottles, goggles and anti-pollution masks. None of us could remember when we last rode a bicycle and that added to the excitement. The only worry I had was that I was a little overweight; I wanted to impress Jazz, which meant I would have to successfully complete the distance.

Wishing I had followed up on my New Year's resolution of not eating junk food, I hoisted myself on to the bicycle. *I'm not sure about the cycle tyres but the tyre around my belly will surely burst*, I thought. Was Randeep serious about covering twenty kilometres on a bicycle? Would they mind if I took a cab instead? I was ready to wait for hours at the destination, as long as I didn't have to pedal all the way there. I thought to myself, *If it wasn't for Jazz, I would throw this cycle into the recycle bin.*

'Are you in love with your cycle? You seem lost,' Jazz asked me as I sat idly on my cycle.

'Oh yeah, this panther is sexy. I'm in love with it. Back when I was in school and in shape I was a champ,' I boasted. *Bad move, bad move!* My mind rang in alarm. *Now she'll have high expectations! Damn it!*

She laughed. I was clueless about whether she was laughing at the joke or at me because I was being stupid. Whatever it was, I couldn't think about it for too long. Without wasting any more time, we set off, with Randeep leading the way, and it made me nostalgic for my schooldays. Life had been so exciting back then. And now? It just seems to fuck me over, left, right and centre. For the first four kilometres I thought, *Okay, this is easy.* Over the next four, I consoled myself thinking, *I can do it. I'm losing calories.* After that I was ready to rest in peace because Jazz was riding right beside me. Instantly, I regained all my energy and pumped up the speed, pretending I was Lance Armstrong, all set to win the next world cycling championship. As I looked at her again, I lost all focus and just drifted alongside. She looked so elegant in her track wear that I wanted to kiss her right there.

Can't we just run away together, just you and me? Just run, hand in hand, and be together for all our days, just you and me? We'll never look back. I'll kiss you and you can have my heart. I'll have your love and you can have mine. It'll be just you and me.

I wanted time to freeze. At least for a little while. Instead, Jazz stopped and got off her bicycle. My heart pumped faster as I wondered why she had stopped. The other three had cycled past us a long time ago while we cruised along the outskirts of Delhi. I got off my cycle and walked up to her.

'Are you okay?' I inquired.

'I just wanted some water.'

I handed her my water bottle without realizing that she too had one. She gave me a surprised look.

'You can have it,' I said, nonchalantly.

She smiled and drank from my bottle while I secretly admired her wet lips and the drops that rolled down her neck. She caught me staring.

'Aren't your eyes going way too low?'

'I'm okay with the top too.'

Slip of the tongue. Fuck! What am I saying? Aditya, control your emotions. Be normal! Shit.

'Bottle top. I meant bottle top. You can have my bottle, I'm okay with the bottle top,' I ranted, hoping to confuse her.

Though I sounded like an idiot, she couldn't control her smile. Was this a green signal? Lacking the courage to ask, I smiled back. As we got back on our cycles, we realized that we had lost track of the route. Neither of our cell phones had network. We tried to guess the correct direction and started moving that way, but it was soon clear that we were lost. The road led to a dead end with dense trees all around, simultaneously peaceful and scary.

'Let's walk with our cycles for a while or let's just sit here for some time. I'm exhausted,' Jazz spoke.

'Thank Heavens,' I murmured.

'Did you say something?' she asked, stretching her legs.

'Nothing.'

'So, you write books,' she said as she took out a wet wipe from her bag.

Wanting to shift the attention away from me on to her, I said, 'Let's talk about ourselves, not about books.' I looked into her eyes. They were mesmerizing.

An awkward silence followed thereafter.

'Are you still angry at what I did?' I asked to break the silence.

'Not really. I trust Priyanshi, and if she feels that you are a nice guy, then I shouldn't be so harsh. All I know is that she won't let me tread the wrong path.'

'I must thank Priyanshi then for guiding you to the right path and leaving us here on the wrong one.' I winked.

She smiled again. *God, that smile!* My stomach turned over each time I saw it.

'Still, I am sorry,' she said.

'I should be sorry for lying to you. We met in a very unconventional manner, but if it wasn't for that, I wouldn't have known you today.' I sat beside her.

'Probably. Do you want a sandwich?' she asked as she unwrapped one.

'Sure. Please pass the water bottle too.'

We looked at each other again and the silence prevailed, but this time it wasn't awkward. It lasted longer than before and we didn't move an inch until I realized my socks were wet. I had spilt all the water from the bottle I was holding.

'You are always in la-la land.' She grinned.

With every passing minute, we grew closer, getting to know each other better. Effortlessly, we talked our hearts out. We laughed. We gossiped. For the first time, I felt like I was really getting to know her, and that was reward enough. I constantly resisted the urge to pinch myself to make sure it was all real, for even if it was a dream, it was one I didn't want to wake up from. Lost in time, we were in the moment, finally together. Our conversation continued ethereally till we saw the rest of the gang cycling towards us. Priyanshi, Dipika and Randeep—I'd completely forgotten about them!

'What's the time?' Jazz asked.

'Shit, we have been here for almost two hours.'

'Really?' She checked her cell phone and was stunned.

'We are so sorry. We got lost and didn't realize it had been so long.' Jazz rained apologies on everyone once they reached us.

'So were you appreciating nature or . . . ?' Randeep teased.

'Shut up,' Jazz snapped at him. She was blushing!

'I stopped to drink water and we lost our way. I was a little tired too and our phones didn't have network,' I said in an attempt to save Jazz from further embarrassment.

'You were drinking water for two long hours?' Priyanshi mused.

'No, it's my fault. I wanted to drink water and then I took a wrong turn,' Jazz said.

'So the blame game has started already? It happens.' Looking at me, Randeep continued in a dramatic, yet comical way, 'You haven't even spent a few hours with her and you've already forgotten your well-wishers? Such is the misery of life!'

Jazz and I glanced at each other and burst out laughing. Whatever had happened that day, it had changed us; we looked at each other differently after that. We were no longer virtual friends, the ones you filter out of your profile once you get bored of them. No, after that day, we became friends in the real sense, and I couldn't have been happier! Jazz had managed to touch my soul in a way that I could never even have dreamed of when I first saw her. She had stolen my heart, and now it was my turn to steal hers.

'Wow, this is amazing! I never knew there were places like this around Delhi,' Dipika exclaimed, as soon as we reached Camp Tikkling.

'It's yet to be explored. But you will remember this forever,' Randeep said. He then went to the manager's office and to discuss certain formalities, while we explored the area. The dark skies and the serenity of nature made the place all the more beautiful. As we unpacked our bags in our tents and settled down, Randeep called us out to start a bonfire and begin barbecuing. Everyone picked a spot around the fire and sat down.

'So Aditya, where do you see yourself in five years?' Randeep asked as he stoked the coal and made drinks for us.

'Five years? That's a tough one. Five years ago, I never would have thought I would quit my management job to write books. Life is about everything clicking into place at the right moment rather than planning for years only to have those plans go awry.'

I sipped my drink and realized everyone was looking at me like I'd said something really thought-provoking. Randeep made another round of drinks and served the chicken along with it.

'What about you?' I bounced the question back at him.

'Simple and sorted. I'll move to the States to earn dollars. The rupee is falling faster than Romeo fell in love with Juliet.' He raised a toast to finding success, and we all cheered.

'Why, this is rare.' Randeep mused. 'The boys are talking and the girls are quiet. How strange. Anyway, where do you see yourself in five years, Priyanshi?'

'As an IAS officer. I just want to clear the UPSC exams this year and start the journey of my dreams.' Priyanshi's voice was calm, yet authoritative.

When Dipika was asked the question, she paused before answering.

'I will be an author. A bestselling author. My books will be in all the stores, in the bestsellers' section, and I'll win everyone's hearts with my words. My parents will be proud. I want to prove to them and to myself that I'm a good writer.'

'That's fascinating! I pray that day comes soon so I can flaunt your autograph and a selfie with you on Facebook.' Priyanshi seemed impressed.

'I'm sure we'll co-author a book someday.' I smiled and added, 'What about you, Jazz?'

Jazz wasn't expecting the attention to shift towards her but when it did, she gulped her drink in one go and said, 'I'll probably be shopping abroad at Louis Vuitton or Jimmy Choo, before relaxing on a beach with a cocktail.'

She laughed but Priyanshi raised an eyebrow. 'Alone?'

'I don't mind if one of you wants to join me in my dream.' She laughed, but I'm sure I heard bells ringing somewhere.

'I'm sure Aditya won't mind joining you,' Dipika whispered, but we could all hear her.

Jazz threw her chicken at her, pretending to be offended, but Dipika caught it with a grin. The drinks continued as the evening grew longer. Once the bottles had nothing left in them and every single one of us was drunk, Dipika and Priyanshi suggested turning on some music to dance. Everyone started swaying to the music and soon a romantic number started playing. We took turns partnering each other. Jazz was a pretty decent dancer; I, on the other hand, was horrible and hoped that the song would end soon to save myself the embarrassment of having to dance with her. My worst fears came true when it was my turn to partner Jazz. There she was, holding my hands and moving her body to the rhythm, while I was hypnotized by the way her face shone under the moonlight. My heart danced more than my legs, the nervousness I felt clearly visible. But I wasn't the only one who was nervous.

Does she love me? She doesn't seem to be showing any signs. Is her nervousness the first sign? Why is it always difficult to know whether a person loves you or not? She is nervous, which must mean she loves me. Yes, nervousness equals love. But I used to get nervous before all my exams. That didn't mean that I loved taking exams. I hated them. Oh fuck. Logically, then, does she hate me?

I was not very good at dancing, but with her, I wanted to dance for a lifetime. I wanted to hold her close to my heart, stop the hands of time and feel our bodies sway together to the music of our heartbeats. I wanted her to open her heart and let me in. She looked enchanting, like a cypress under the moonlight, in her sparkling pink dress. Her smile could have made the gods envious. She seemed to effortlessly glide, not missing a beat.

The rhythm of the moment,
Moving to a beat,
My activity,
Her receptivity.
I felt the sweat on her back.
A couple of minutes and the song was over.
Inebriated from the feeling of love in the air,
And with the help of drinks,
He addressed her.
Would you like to dance?

His voice exposed his inexperience at these types of things.
Their naked hands meet,
Her soft skin contains the power to heal.
Suddenly, his life makes sense.
Today he lost a game,
But gained a soulmate.

For a few brief minutes, we forgot about the world that existed around us. We were lost in the moment, charged with emotions and the effects of alcohol. While her emotions were still hidden and wrapped under a thick layer of protection, mine waited at the doorstep of her heart. Love is strange. It's a feeling that can't be expressed in words, but is completely understood by the person it is meant for. And in some rare cases, when the lover is lucky and deserving enough, this love is reciprocated.

While everyone slept, I was falling in love. Growing up, I had always thought that dreams were just dreams, and that nightmares couldn't hurt you. I believed that those dreams and nightmares were harmless, that they were just something your subconscious mind conjured up. But my dreams of being with Jazz in the near future directly affected my sleep. I got out of my sleeping blanket and walked outside the tent for a walk, hoping it would tire me out. To my surprise, I saw Jazz sitting on a bench, gazing up at the sky.

'Hey . . . couldn't sleep?' she asked, as I sat next to her.

'You don't seem too happy seeing me here. Should I go then?' I teased.

'No, stay. I just wasn't expecting anyone to be awake.' She looked a little embarrassed.

She moved aside to make space for me. Our closeness spoke a thousand words, but it wasn't the exact closeness that I longed for. I wanted her arms around me as tight as possible, uncaring of whether I could breathe.

'Can I ask you something? If you don't mind,' I whispered.

She just stared at me but didn't object so I proceeded. 'Is there anything that haunts you?'

She looked away, lost in her thoughts.

Should I move few inches closer? It might be a bit too much. An inch won't harm anyone though. Should I put my arms around her? No! Too much, too soon.

Her aroma was intoxicating. It sent my senses for a toss. I closed my eyes to feel her presence around me. Just meeting someone's gaze for the first time does not constitute love at first sight. It's when you *can't* bring yourself to look away from them that you know you're in love. You fear that when you avert your eyes, the magical moment will be a thing of the past—the eyes you were looking at moments ago will carry on with their life, and the thought scares you. I was overwhelmed by a numbness I couldn't explain, till she turned to me and looked intently into my eyes.

'I want to be with someone who will love me the way I am and accept my wishes.'

'And what are those?' I asked.

'I want to start something of my own and I want to adopt a child.'

'Adopt?'

'Yeah, even if I have kids of my own, I want to adopt one.'

She looked at me, her gaze unsure. An inexplicable silence followed. The quietness around us and the serenity within us defined our emotions.

'Have you ever told this to your parents or close friends?'

'No. No one yet.' She confessed.

'So I am the first to know this?' I was surprised.

'Yes.'

'Why?' I asked, shocked and yet happy that she had trusted me with something so important.

'I don't know. There is no reason.'

'There must be something.' I pushed.

'I just felt like telling you.' She smiled.

'Thank you. Your secret is safe with me. I feel loved by your kindness,' I confessed.

'Why?' Now it was her turn to be surprised.

'I don't know. There is no reason.'

'There must be something?' She persisted.

'I just felt like it.' I smirked.

Jazz had come into my life unexpectedly and everything had changed, taking a turn for the better. Her warm eyes, her laugh, the sincerity in her voice and her kindness, they all had become an inseparable part of my life. As she revealed her real self to me, I happily discovered more and more beauty in her. I was amazed to find so much gentleness in one person. Without even knowing it, she had made a place for herself in my heart. There was no more pretence left, and now it had become that much easier to just be with her.

Dipika and I returned to Mumbai the following day, but I was leaving my heart in Delhi. Jazz had stolen my heart before I could even say anything and now it was hers to keep forever.

Dream: Shutting Down Permanently

Two months later . . .

The best relationships usually begin unexpectedly. Even though Jazz, Dipika, Randeep, Priyanshi and I were in different cities, we maintained an emotional connection with each other. Also, technology never let us realize we were away from each other. Sometimes we even had Skype parties: everyone would log into their Skype accounts and have drinks. It sounded ridiculous to other people; they wouldn't understand, because they weren't us.

Randeep's visa had been approved and he was currently in the process of completing other formalities. He was very close to achieving his dream. Priyanshi had taken her UPSC exams and was anxiously awaiting the results. It was her last attempt to clear the hurdle. Randeep's decision to move to the US gave Priyanshi's parents another chance to taunt her about her 'failures' because, according to them, she was doing nothing productive.

We all stood by her and encouraged her as much as we could. Randeep was the one who consoled her whenever she was sad. Jazz was her morale booster. Priyanshi often said that both of them were her lifeline; without them, she would collapse. Meanwhile, Dipika was waiting to hear from the publishers she had sent her manuscript to. She had submitted it a week after returning from Delhi. She had emailed the publishers several times but to no effect, and this was really starting to worry her.

It's said that one person can change your outlook towards life, and Jazz was proving that true for me. She had made me a better person—far more calm, composed and mature than I had been before. As the days passed, she was promoted at the Sun Group where she was working as a business development manager, and my new book was ready to hit the market.

As for us, we were not just friends. There was definitely something more developing between us, but neither of us wanted to acknowledge it openly, thus prolonging the inevitable. We loved talking to each other, sending locations and live updates through WhatsApp messages and emojis on Facebook.

Every time she felt me slipping away, she extended her hand, reaching out just far enough for our fingertips to touch, granting me hope. But then she'd pull back. She never wanted me to be too close, but she didn't want me too far away either. Some people enter our lives and become an integral part of it in such a short period that it makes us wonder if it's really true. Often, Jazz and I would Skype all night, turning off other distractions; we would watch TV shows together; we'd send each other audio messages and selfies on WhatsApp all through the day. We were two humans, but two halves of the same soul. Separated by distance, but we were never alone. Kilometres apart, but it was only a matter of time before we embraced each other as one.

It was a lazy afternoon. Jazz had just woken up after her late shift the previous night and I decided to lighten her mood on WhatsApp.

Me: *Hi, remember me?*

She freshened up and walked towards the kitchen, mobile in hand. She read the message and replied.

Jazz: *Yes, so?*
Me: *My life revolves around you. *kiss**
Jazz: *Then please give me a life. I really can't wait any more.*

Me: *Are you serious? This is what I have been waiting for! *heart**

Jazz: *Yes, I too can't wait any more. Time's running out and I'm at level 100, still waiting for someone to give me a life. *sad**

Me: *Are you trying to troll me? *thinks**

Jazz: *Not trying, succeeding. Ha ha!*

Me: *Hate you. *devil**

Jazz: *Who said that I love you?*

Me: *Your 'last seen' status on WhatsApp.*

Jazz: *What?*

Me: *You don't sleep these days because you're thinking about me. *angel**

Jazz: *Don't you think you've been acting too smart these days?*

Me: *Acting? I am! But the girl I love is slightly smarter. I tried to mock her but was mocked instead.*

Jazz: *Poor you. *kiss**

Me: *And lucky her.*

Jazz: *angry*

Me: *Why are you so afraid of love?*

Jazz: *Oh, I almost forgot! I'm coming to Mumbai next week.*

Me: *Awesome! Let's go on a date.*

Jazz: *Why? You aren't my boyfriend. *wink**

I was about to reply when someone rang the doorbell. I got up to see who had interrupted our love story. It was Dipika, whose expression changed from jovial to annoyed as soon as she saw me still in my boxers and slippers.

'Shit, I completely forgot!' I had promised to go shopping with her.

'I'll give you five minutes,' she warned.

'Promise, next time I'll come for sure!' I tried pleading with her.

'You're not to be trusted.' She saw through me.

'Pinky promise. Jazz promise!' I did my best to avoid going. I wanted to stay home and continue my conversation with Jazz.

'Fine then. I'm sure you're chatting with Jazz. It's the only time you butter me up this much.'

'You are so smart.' I winked.

'You are impossible. Bye!' She left without closing the door.

'I promise, next time. Jazz promise,' I called after her.

Dipika had emailed Mr Roy, her publisher, several times after their meeting in Delhi, in the hope of getting a reply, but every time she refreshed her email, she found no new mail from him. It had turned into a daily routine for her, but she was left with no other option, so she continued doing so.

She was miffed with Mr Roy for not responding to all of her calls, messages and emails. Her hopes sank with each passing day. After shopping, she spotted a bookstore in the mall and thought of looking up some new publishers she could send her manuscript, starting all over again. She glanced at the racks of books and the names of their authors. Whenever she came across a title in her genre she noted down the publisher's name. After flipping through the pages of a few books, she moved on to the new releases section. All the latest releases were piled one on top of the other. She started reading from the top, carefully looking through each title, when one of the staff approached her.

'Are you looking for any particular title, ma'am?'

'Not really, I am here to note down the names of a few publishers. I am an aspiring writer and I want to publish my book.'

'Wow. I think I can help you with that. Give me a few minutes.'

He went to the counter and started looking for something on his computer while Dipika turned back to the books. Wading through the titles, she saw something that shocked the living daylights out of her. She felt as if her world had stopped. Her knees felt wobbly and, although she knew it was true, she hoped that it was all just a bad dream. In the new releases section, she came across a book with the same title she had used for her own novel, the one that she had sent to Mr Roy. She flipped through the pages; it was very similar to her story. In fact, even the climax was no different from hers. She realized then that Mr Roy had fed her lies—he was not who he claimed to be. She remembered him talking about publishing etiquette. The minute Dipika had let her guard down, it was all over. He had stolen her manuscript and published it under someone else's name. *That lying bastard!* she cursed in her head. Dipika was shattered.

She ran to the counter with the book, and the salesperson immediately sensed that something was gravely wrong.

'What is it, ma'am? Are you okay?' He left the counter to get her a glass of water.

'When . . . ah . . . when was this book released?' Dipika stammered.

'This Sunday. We just put it on display. Is there anything wrong with it?' he asked curiously.

'Yes. Everything is wrong with it.'

'Meaning?' The salesman looked confused.

'The author. They didn't write this book.'

Without waiting for the salesman to respond, Dipika left the store and called Mr Roy, but there was no answer. In this unfair world, the powerful had yet again asserted their might, exploiting the weak. Dipika regretted her decision to keep her plans a secret until the book was published.

I wish I'd at least told Aditya about it. He has experience in this field. Fuck, man, this is so not done.

How could Mr Roy just misuse my hard work? Shit, I'm such an idiot for trusting him and submitting the entire manuscript without any paperwork. I am so screwed. My hard work, my sleepless nights, my words, my characters, my story, my dream—all gone. I should call Aditya right away. But how am I going to tell him? Maybe I should leave him a text . . .

Dipika took out her cell phone and composed a long message.

Aditya, it's all over. I shouldn't have kept this hidden from you. I regret it so much now. I lost it. If I had had even the slightest clue, I wouldn't have taken a step without your approval. Mr Roy, the publisher? I'm sure you know him very well. That bastard lied to me and stole my book! I wanted to surprise you, Jazz and the others. I was just in a bookstore and I saw my story and title under somebody else's name in the new releases section. How the fuck could he do this to me? I've been working on that manuscript for such a long time. How can someone just steal someone's hard work like this, knowing the effort an author puts into shaping a manuscript? I feel insulted, Aditya. I don't think I'll ever write again—I have no courage left. I really want to sue Mr Roy but I have no paperwork to prove that the manuscript was mine. Just a few drafts

are not going to help. My dream has been sunk; it lies
deep in the ocean of betrayal, and I don't know if I'll
ever recover from this blow.

Dejected, Dipika went home and locked herself in the darkness of her room. There were no physical wounds to reveal her pain, but her heart was broken. When dreams shatter they make no noise. Only the sounds of fallen tears prevail.

When I received Dipika's message, I immediately rushed to her house to find out the entire truth, and hearing it left me doleful. She was inconsolable, just like a child whose toy had been stolen. You can always give the child a new toy to bring a smile to his face, but a dream once stolen cannot be bought again. Things wouldn't have turned out like this had she at least discussed it with me once. I wanted to scream at her for keeping me out of the loop, but that wouldn't solve anything now. I racked my brain about what we could do next, for she had no legal documents apart from a few emails to prove her story. I assured her that I would take care of it, but, in all truthfulness, I had no idea whether it was really possible.

Could this be the end of her writing career? Was it going to crash-land like this, before it even had the chance to take off? If not, how was she supposed to claim her rights with no valid proof or paperwork?

July 2015
Bandra

The struggles of life and the battles to freely express ourselves had changed us all. As I sipped water from my glass to compose myself, Jazz held Dipika's hand. Recalling the moment when Dipika had learnt of her betrayal, I remembered how heartbroken she had been. Even now, she couldn't control her tears. Time had definitely put some distance between the initial hurt and devastation that Dipika had felt, but it could not heal the ugly scars she had been left with. The trauma of that incident had left a lasting impression on her, so much so that whenever she remembered it, she felt like a part of her life was slipping away. It wasn't easy for her to cope, but she did so anyway for the sake of her friends who wanted to see her smile. In the beginning, she hated even looking at books. Such was the intensity of her hurt. What made it worse was that she had stopped writing as well. Roma was still processing everything she had heard so far.

'Di, why did you hide all this from me? I'm your sister and I was in the dark! You didn't do anything? You let him get away with it?' Roma asked in frustration.

'No. We did everything possible.'

'Did anything come of it then?'

'He was powerful and ran a fake publishing house. I knew this well before Dipika told me, and as soon as she did, I knew it was going to be nasty. Using my sources, I collected all the necessary documents in the following days, and with a copy of the emails that they had exchanged, we landed up at his office in Delhi without notice. He looked like he'd seen a ghost! I showed him all the evidence we had and laid out a clear case in front of him. I also slapped him, figuratively, with a legal notice and gave him an official letter pointing out that he had violated an ethical code.

'Then?' Roma asked, stupefied.

'He was left with no option but to halt printing of the new editions to save his reputation. But Dipika didn't want to take the legal route. Her parents were vehemently against it and she respected their decision. But because of the trauma, Dipika quit writing. Even after my continuous attempts to convince her to resume, she remains stubborn. I tried to make her understand that such situations occur and that I too had faced them initially, but she has never recovered from it.'

'But why?' Roma asked a teary-eyed Dipika.

'Because I had no choice. We tried everything possible. Filing a case against him not only meant disturbing our own mental peace but also losing a lot of money. Dad felt the same way. He knew that in the years to come, even if we won the case, we would lose our time and sanity because of the mental harassment that bastard would put us through. Even then, once we were assured that he had stopped subsequent printings of my book, I resent the manuscript to other publishers. But many didn't respond, and the ones who did rejected the manuscript as it had already made its debut in the market. It isn't easy writing a book. Eventually, I got busy with my life and I lost interest. Even though Roy never published another book again, he impaired my ability to publish. I couldn't get myself to write again.'

In my opinion, Dipika shouldn't have let that incident affect her deeply enough to stop writing, but she couldn't be convinced otherwise. She had other things to focus on as well, which made it easier for her to give up writing. Life becomes a little easier when you have options to choose from. But at the same time, it dilutes the worth of struggling for that one goal without which life will never be the same. Such is the strangeness of life. It brings us excruciating pain and then, with time, it teaches us to move on. Nothing and no one can make you feel better when you've been knocked down by life, but each day makes you a better person.

'Even now, I push her to write but she has a lot of advice to give me instead,' I teased.

'And you don't value that either.' Dipika tried to smile.

'But I do value it!' I protested.

'Cut the crap.' She laughed.

'But I really do. Which is why we are still friends.'

Roma was about to ask something when the waiter interrupted us. 'May I refill your glass?'

'Nah, that's okay,' Dipika replied.

'We take our last order at midnight. So if you want something from the kitchen, please do order before that,' the waiter informed us. Jazz glanced at her watch.

'It's only ten now. We'll order a little later,' Jazz said, and the waiter left.

'What happened to your story?' Roma moved her chair a little closer towards me.

'Our story?' I repeated.

'Yes. How did it start finally? Did she propose or did you take the initiative?'

'She did.' I winked at Jazz.

'What the fuck? You are such a liar,' Jazz exclaimed.

'What? Who gave the first signal then?' I raised an eyebrow at her.

'Oh really? You were the one who was dying to ask me out from the beginning.'

'To be fair, I was a little hesitant about whether a long-distance relationship would work. People fight over 'last seen' statuses on WhatsApp despite living in the same city, and there she was, living over a thousand kilometres away. But then she initiated it and I followed.' I winked again.

'Oh, fuck off.' Jazz laughed.

Roma looked anxious to know more, so I continued.

Admit It, You Love Me

True love exceeds the boundaries of your heart and seeps into your soul. We wait for it to happen accidentally but the wait never ends. Sometimes we think too much and lose sight of it. Although I hadn't known Jazz for long, we had nothing to conceal from each other. Strangely, we were dissimilar in a lot of ways. She was from Delhi, I from Mumbai. She was a Sikh, I was a Brahmin. We were like a poem whose lines didn't rhyme but our togetherness had meaning, which made everything worth it. Her presence added happiness to my life and my presence made her smile. Love isn't always like a lightning bolt; it doesn't happen in a split second. It's just a decision, a decision to take a chance with somebody without worrying about whether they'll give anything back or if they'll hurt you or if they are really the one. Sometimes it jumps at you from around the corner when you're least expecting it; other times it's a conscious choice that you make.

I had made my decision a long time ago and I didn't expect anything from Jazz in return. There were so many ways for me to say what I wanted to say to her, thousands of words to choose from, but I still didn't know how to start. Mustering all my courage, I messaged her . . .

Me: *Do you think long-distance relationships work?*

She didn't reply for a while and I stared at my mobile screen. As her WhatsApp status changed from online to typing, my heartbeat quickened. Fingers crossed, I fervently hoped for an affirmative reply.

Jazz: *I don't know. But it's not easy for sure. We cannot meet often, share our feelings often. Moreover, trusting each other is one hell of a task.*

I jumped out of bed when I read 'we'. Did she mean *our* relationship or was she just quoting an example? Whatever it was, it made me curious and I immediately responded.

Me: *We? Do you mean . . .*
I purposely kept it open-ended to see her reaction.
Jazz: *Just because.*
Me: *But 'we'. WHY?*
Jazz: *I don't know.*

93

Me: *But there must be something.*
Jazz: *I just felt so. *smiles**

Was I overthinking and getting ahead of myself, or did she really mean it? I was clueless but the suspense was too much for me. I was still in Delhi to clear Dipika's case with the publisher and was going to leave for Mumbai the following day with Jazz who had an official meeting in the city. Dipika had decided to stay back in Delhi for a couple of days to keep an eye on the stock that was being returned to the publisher. I wanted to take this opportunity to go all out and reveal my feelings. I replied to Jazz's message.

I don't think I should suppress my feelings any more. I don't know if it's the right time but no one ever knows when it is the right time to do anything. I've kept these feelings hidden for too long now. Having known each other for the past couple of months, you and I are no longer strangers. You probably know by now what I intend to say to you, but give me the opportunity to say this to you in person tomorrow. I don't know whether we will share the same bond once the bubble bursts, but it's imperative that you know. I can't hold it any longer.

I loved her; she would have to be blind not to have seen it by now. I earlier thought it was her external beauty but then I soon realized that it wasn't just her face, but the expressions on her face that made my heart beat faster. I had made up my mind. I knew that things would never be the same again but that's what life is about—taking risks! There's more to life than just sitting around waiting for something to happen; life will then just pass us by.

'What's happened to you? You're smiling like a maniac!' Priyanshi asked as she changed the TV channel.

As Priyanshi put her favourite show on mute to listen to the details, Jazz told her about the conversation that had ensued between the two of us that morning. As Jazz showed her the chats and the last message, Priyanshi cried out in happiness.

'I can assure you of one thing, he loves you like no one's loved before. The way he pampers you and makes you smile, no one can match that. I don't know what is stopping you from taking it forward. But you are very lucky, Jazz.'

'I sometimes wonder whether you are my friend or his,' Jazz accused playfully, snatching the phone from her.

'He is my *jiju*,' Priyanshi teased.

'Shut up!' Jazz said, throwing a pillow at her.

Turning serious for a moment, Priyanshi asked, 'Tell me honestly though, do you not have any feelings for him?'

'I don't know,' Jazz replied.

'Stop giving me lame answers. I'm asking you very seriously. He's going to propose to you when you travel together tomorrow. I just know it. So you should have an answer ready by then.' Priyanshi sat upright, holding the pillow tightly.

'It's just that . . .' Jazz hesitated.

'What?'

Jazz put her phone aside and said, 'He is nice, but he's also very different from me. We have nothing in common. His lifestyle is different from mine. Worst of all is the fact that we'd have to be in a long-distance relationship. We chat, we interact, but being in a relationship, especially when you're in different states, is different and difficult. I'm afraid to be in love. You know that.'

'So you do like him?'

'It's not about whether I like him or not. I'm trying to explain to you how I feel! Even if I like him, loving him and committing to him is a different story altogether. I am not ready for that. Not right now, at least.'

'Okay, fine. But you don't hate him, right?' Through different ways, Priyanshi was trying to get the one answer she wanted to hear from Jazz.

'I don't. But if you don't hate someone, it doesn't mean that you love them either. I am not sure, and everything is scary. I don't want to get hurt in the future.'

'So you will reject him if he proposes tomorrow?'

'I haven't thought about it, to be honest.'

Both of them looked at each other in silence. Priyanshi tried to search for the love that she knew Jazz harboured secretly in her heart while Jazz just stared blankly into space, thinking hard about Priyanshi's questions. She had no answer. Or was she trying to run away from reality? She was definitely somewhere in between. She was in two minds about whether the whole thing could ever work out. What if it didn't and she lost herself in the process? What if after rejection she realizes it had been love, after all? Some people live in a state of confusion their entire lives, in search of love, and some, despite finding it, don't value it until it's gone.

'I think it's late. We should sleep,' Jazz announced. She had contemplated enough for one day.

Before going to sleep, Priyanshi turned to Jazz. 'It's still not too late. Accept him before it does get too late. I have seen a positive change in you since Aditya has stepped into your life. You smile more often and your happiness knows no bounds. I don't understand why you won't acknowledge it. He genuinely loves you and is ready to accept you the way you are. What else do you want? Trust me, he will make all your dreams come true. It's not that you can't do it yourself, but he's the kind of guy who will stand by you. Don't lose him because you fear the uncertain.'

Jazz nodded but didn't reply. She was still not convinced and believed that this phase would pass. She couldn't see a sweet poem taking birth, holding meaning. She feared love and had stayed away from it all her life, living in denial. But was she in denial about her true feelings? She had very little time to figure it out.

Should I give her a hint? Or should I wait for the right moment to arrive? I should give her something that she can flaunt for a lifetime, I thought to myself, as I sat beside Jazz, waiting for the flight to take off.

Is he really going to propose? Priyanshi was confident he would. We'll be sitting next to each other for the next two hours. If the last two months weren't sufficient time for me to decide, then how can I possibly decide in these two hours? What if he proposes now? Fuck! Such were the thoughts that an anxious Jazz was grappling with.

She looked at me and flashed an awkward smile.

I think she expects it. I should tell her. I returned her awkward smile.

'I . . . I think you . . .'

Before I could say anything further, she interrupted me. 'Could you give me two hours?'

'Two hours? For what?'

She realized that her thoughts were racing faster than reality and tried to cover up for her incoherence.

'Oh sorry. I meant could you give me your portable charger for two hours. My phone is running out of battery.'

I understood her anxiety, which made me empathetic, and I decided to wait till the end of the journey to confess my feelings. The right words at the right moment with the right people can give one a lifetime of happy memories and I was waiting to become a part of her memory and, in the process, make a few shared memories. As the seat belt sign was switched off, Jazz closed her eyes to take a nap. In the meantime, I gazed at her beauty. Deeply asleep, her head tilted towards me and rested on my shoulder. Unsure of how to react, I let her sleep like that and, once in a while, I ran my fingers through her hair. I wanted the aircraft to stay in the air forever so she could stay this close to me for eternity. I didn't want to let go of her.

As I played with Jazz's hair, she sensed it and woke up, looking into my eyes. Our breath mingled and our lips touched. We didn't care if the airhostesses or our fellow passengers witnessed our moment of intimacy, we continued exploring each other's mouths. An announcement to fasten our seat belts woke me up, which is when I realized that I had dozed, my mind full of thoughts about her. She was still soundly asleep on my shoulder.

'Jazz,' I whispered softly. She groaned. 'Wake up. We have landed.'

She awoke with a jerk, realizing that she had been resting on my shoulder all this while. She gave me an embarrassed smile. As we deboarded the aircraft, I rushed to the washroom to make a call. Not a call of nature but a telephone call to confirm whether my proposal plan was on schedule and to check if the car had arrived outside. Once I was done, I went to the luggage belt where Jazz was waiting. She had no idea what was coming her way.

As we emerged from the airport and sat in the car, Jazz asked, 'How long will it take to reach the hotel?'

'We are going somewhere else,' I muttered, fearing her reaction.

'Somewhere else? When was that decided?' Jazz questioned.

'We didn't decide. I did.'

'What?'

'Yes.' I looked at her betrayed expression.

'Are you serious?'

'As a heart attack.'

A dead silence followed all the way till the outskirts of Mumbai. Jazz was anxious to know where we were heading but didn't ask any questions. In a way, I was glad. The lush green valley made for an idyllic view as the car sped away.

'This is the expressway. We're going to Lonavla,' I informed her.

She remained expressionless. I wished I had the skill to read her poker face.

'We will return late in the afternoon. Don't worry. Your meetings are all scheduled for tomorrow,' I assured her.

'That doesn't mean—' she began.

Cutting her short, I said, 'I know. But trust me anyway.'

Love gives you an adrenaline rush that makes all your senses come alive, turning your world around. As we approached our destination, I became more nervous by the minute. We hadn't stopped anywhere during the journey. Jazz had no idea what lay ahead of her. I'd booked a hot-air balloon ride for us in Lonavla. I wanted to give her the experience of a lifetime. Upon reaching our destination, the manager of the adventure company welcomed us with a big bouquet of flowers and a card that read:

It's going to be an exceptional day with Aditya. Are you ready? Feel it and live it.

The manager started preparing the balloon. Jazz couldn't believe her eyes and I could tell from her stunned expression that she was quite excited. There were some mixed feelings too, but hopefully, after today, they'd all go away. I wanted to do something that no one had ever done for her, something that brought a smile to her face—that was enough for me. She continued to maintain her silence but I sensed a change in her attitude. She was no longer impatient, letting things take their own sweet time, setting the atmosphere for the perfect romantic date that I'd always envisioned with her.

'I know what you are thinking, but trust me, you will love it,' I said, taking hold of her hand.

She glanced at our interlocked fingers and asked, 'But why all this?'

She had a childlike grin on her face which I'd never seen before. I paused for a moment before slowly whispering in her ears, 'Are you pretending or do you really not know?' I smiled.

There was no reaction from her but my question made her blush. That's all the answer I needed. Sometimes expressions speak more than actions and hers said it all.

The crew guided us to the launch site. The basket and balloon were laid out so that the wind aided the inflation process. We looked at each other but no words were exchanged—we needed none to express the exhilaration we felt, it was evident on our faces. The period of innocence before expressing your love to someone is always endearing. She looked so radiant that my heart softened and a smile played constantly on my lips. She was the most exquisite human being I had ever laid eyes on. She was like an addiction for me, seductive as hell; like a good book, she was fascinating to the core; like a novel idea, she was a breath of fresh air; and like music, her mere presence was soothing.

When the balloon was finally full of air, the pilot lit the burner and brought the balloon upright. It was time to climb on board.

'I'm scared,' Jazz confessed.

I squeezed her hand to reassure her, and she held on tight, climbing into the basket.

'Are you sure you still want to do this?' she asked and I nodded. And then off we went!

We both gasped loudly as we bid goodbye to land. Once we got over the initial fear of floating in the air, we focused on the view from the top—it was breathtaking. The landscape, the valley, the sky. Maybe it was her, maybe it was the freshness of the air, but a part of me never wanted to go back down again. A part of me wanted to stay there forever, in the middle of a limitless sky full of possibilities. Once we felt comfortable, I held her by her waist and pulled towards me. She was taken aback for a second but soon shied away. Her eyes were closed and there was no space for air between us. Once again, I gently grabbed her waist and hugged her. As she wrapped her hands around me, she melted in my arms. I was still not sure whether it was the fear of heights that got to her or whether it was the love she had, but the moment had arrived, and I knew it was the right moment. It couldn't have been more perfect. The cool breeze and serene beauty around us were definitely a sign from the universe. I had to tell her. It was either now or never.

'I have to tell you something,' I whispered.

She looked at me curiously, her eyes searching mine for an answer.

'You have given me a reason to smile again. We might be poles apart but I know that what we have is something special. You're my first thought in the morning and my last thought at night and every thought in between. You don't have to say a word; I just want to be with you. You've shown me how to dream again and you've shown me how to feel again. My friends think I am crazy but all I think is I'm privileged to even know you. When I look at you, I get goosebumps. No doubt, you are beautiful and I can't explain how I feel about you, but meeting you has changed my life. You gave me a chance to be your friend and the day I saw you, I was mesmerized. Your voice left me enchanted and the feeling of love didn't let me sleep the whole night. I wondered if I was all right only to realize later that I love you . . . like crazy. You mean everything to me. Nothing in this world will exist if you are not a part of it. I know you think that long-distance relationships don't work but if you are with right person, they do. Distance may discourage our love, but I promise that I'll always love you, against all odds.'

Jazz hugged me once again and we blew our insecurities into the air and promised each other that we'd be together always. For no matter how different we were from each other, we found solace in each other's arms and that was something worth fighting for. Finding the perfect partner is never easy. Jazz was the best and it wasn't just because she was beautiful. The way she made me laugh, inspired and supported me through the good and the bad, deserved to be appreciated. Her friendship meant so much to me that I couldn't help falling in love with her. I gave her a short note that I had written for her.

> There was a huge void in my life until you came along. You complete me. I think back to how empty my life was without you and I am so grateful that you are here now. I can't wait to spend forever with you. You are my life, my love, my soulmate, my heart and my very reason for breathing. I love you with everything that I am.

On reading it, Jazz looked into my eyes and said, 'I couldn't have asked for more. You make me feel special, as if I am the only one for you. Seeing you happy and knowing I'm the reason for it makes me feel special. I get angry and show that I don't care but on the other end of the cell phone screen you have no idea how I feel. I care about you so much. You are a wonderful person and I'd be honoured to be with you. You're your own person and that's what I love about you.

Whenever I have a bad day, you always make sure I go to bed smiling. I know that as long as you are by my side, I'll be okay through every struggle. When I look at you . . . I see my life. You understand me and you know how to make things just right. You will never know just how much you mean to me, but I will spend the rest of my days trying to show you just that. I thank Waheguruji for bringing us together. I love you . . . and I will continue to love you forever.'

The winds were calm and the balloon rested on the ground safely, marking the beginning of our love life. The post-flight celebrations were set up on a portable table with champagne and a card that the manager held.

He loves you like no one can. Just love him like no one can. Keep all your rights reserved for each other.

Neither of us could have imagined coming this far when I had first sent a friend request to her. We threw all our sorrows and pain into the darkness of our past and claimed our long-lost smiles. She had been in the custody of fear for years but love broke all the shackles that held her heart, letting her experience magic for the first time in a long time. If our love could have been captured in a movie, I would watch it every day, and if it were a dream, I would hope for the same dream every night.

Love Installed Successfully in Our Lives

There are only two probable outcomes when we express our love—either they will become the words of your love poems or you'll end up holding your loved one's hands in yours. I fell in the latter category, as she held my hand in the back seat of the car. I had been in a daze ever since we had landed. When it comes to love, the truth can't remain hidden for too long. Love is abused, cursed and badmouthed, but when you find the person who has potential to love you truly, you start loving love. Both Jazz and I had gone through the worst experiences with love in our lives, to a point where we had started to believe love had boycotted us and that maybe we were meant to live our lives alone, forever. But the Fates had other plans. Because when we were least expecting it, love entered our lives and matched our souls with one other's. With open arms, we embraced this feeling. Life isn't about cribbing about the past but about accepting what comes your way with grace. Our love story had finally taken off!

'You know, we owe our relationship and happiness to Mark,' I said.

'Mark? Mark who?'

'Mark Zuckerberg. If it wasn't for Facebook, I wouldn't have come across your picture and you wouldn't have added Aadi.' I laughed.

'You're crazy. My kind of crazy.' She blushed.

As we reached the outskirts of Mumbai, I asked the driver to slow down near McDonald's to get some burgers and fries. We were already late, as I had to pick up my car and drop Jazz off at the hotel. She insisted on going for a drive in my car. Taking the cab we were in to the hotel was a convenient option but you cannot say no to your girlfriend, especially on your first day as an official couple!

'You should eat less junk food. It's not good for your health and makes you unfit,' Jazz suggested, munching enthusiastically on her fries.

'Is that applicable only to me?' I asked, pointing towards the fries in her hand.

'Maybe,' Jazz sang and took a big bite of her burger. Damn, I love a girl who can eat!

Everything about her drove me crazy—her looks, her voice, even the way she ate. It may sound silly, but when you are in a relationship, your logic goes for a toss.

We picked up my car and drove to Bandra Kurla Complex, where her hotel was located. I stopped by the side of the road, casually starting a conversation to prolong saying goodbye to her for the day. It was pretty dark outside and the weather was taking a turn for the worse. I rolled up the windows and looked at her. She seemed a little nervous, as was I, for we could both feel the tension and energy rise up around us. It was dark outside, with romantic music playing in the car and the windows up. We waited in anticipation for what would come next. Who would have thought that at a moment as perfect that this, someone would rain on our parade? We heard a knock on the window and when I turned to take a look, there they stood, trying to peek in. Notorious for their timing, it was the Mumbai police.

'What happened, sir?' I asked sliding the window down.

'Come out . . . What's happening here?' The policeman asked as he bent to see Jazz sitting next to me. She wore a scared expression on her face.

'Don't worry. You sit inside. I'll handle it,' I assured Jazz as I stepped out of the car.

'Please don't mess with them,' she pleaded.

With a nod, I got out and asked, 'What's wrong, kaka?'

There were two policemen. I looked towards the other and repeated, 'What happened, Uncle?'

Sensing trouble, the shift from 'sir' to 'uncle' didn't take much time. They were keenly observing my body language and the car, clearly using their twisted formula to calculate how much money they could extract from me.

'Where do you stay?' one of them asked with a heavy voice.

'The car is registered in Mumbai,' I clarified.

'Where do you stay?' This time he raised his voice.

I peeped inside to check if Jazz was all right and answered, 'Thane.'

'What are you doing here?'

'I was dropping my friend home.' I didn't reveal the fact that she was from Delhi to avoid complications.

The cops came closer to my mouth and ordered me to speak my name to test whether I was drunk.

'He is drunk,' declared one of them.

'What the . . . No, Uncle, you can test me using the machine.' I controlled my temper before it got me into further trouble.

'Where is the girl from?'

I suppose Jazz heard that and came out of the car in fear. She probably noticed the change in my temperament.

'Delhi,' she answered.

The cops stared at me strangely. I knew I was screwed but I pretended as if I was the most innocent guy on the planet.

'The car is from Mumbai and the girl from Delhi?' His tone changed.

'Sir, you don't have the right to talk like that with a woman present. You can talk to me, clarify any issues with me and take my licence if I have done anything wrong. But we were only talking and the last time I checked, that wasn't a crime. I have not parked illegally either. So please, I'd appreciate it if you calmed down a little.'

That was it. The flame I had been suppressing blazed out, ignited to a full fury at their disrespectful behaviour towards Jazz. I calmly asked her to get back in the car and advised her not to come out. This wasn't something new for a Mumbaikar. Taking advantage of the common man's fear, the police have always tried to assert their dominance but before they could do so, I tackled the situation diplomatically. As they left, I went back inside the car and hugged Jazz who was shivering with fear.

'You don't need to be scared of such people when I'm with you,' I said, as I tried to calm her.

'Did you pay them?' she asked feebly.

'Not even a paisa. Speaking Marathi worked just fine. You should learn it soon to handle such situations.'

'Shut up. I don't want to.' She gave a small smile.

'You don't want to learn Marathi or you don't want to handle such situations?' I teased.

'Bye. I hate you,' she said dramatically.

'But I love you.'

'I don't,' she said, keeping her distance.

'You do,' I insisted.

'Get lost.'

'You're stuck with me now. Forever!' She laughed as soon as I said that. In a way, it was true, and I couldn't have been happier!

Jazz was busy the next day with her meetings. We had a long late-night conversation, after which we dozed off. But not before deciding to meet in the morning. As I reached her hotel, I called her from the lobby asking her to come down but she requested me to come up to her room instead as she was still in the process of getting ready. She opened the door and gave me a warm but brief hug.

'Aditya, I want coffee,' Jazz declared.

'So let's go have some,' I suggested.

'No, I want it now. Right now,' she insisted.

'Okay, let me order it.' I reached for the phone by the bed.

'No. I want it now,' she repeated.

'So what should I do?'

'Make it.'

Alas, the welcome hug was the only pleasant part of the morning and then the unpleasantness soon followed. Step by step, she instructed me on how to make coffee, while she relaxed in bed. After my first attempt at making coffee, I tasted it before handing it to her. It was the worst cup of coffee I'd ever tasted! Even so, she took the cup from me and drank it, without a single complaint. She wasn't kidding anyone, I knew it tasted like crap, which is exactly what I told her, to which she replied, 'For me, it's not about the taste. It's about the effort you made to make me happy. I love you.'

'But you don't need to drink pathetic coffee to prove your love to me, although I'm very flattered.' I winked.

I tried to snatch the cup away but she insisted that she wanted to finish it. Perhaps, it was an attempt to convey that if she ever made an unpalatable dish, I would have to return the favour. I didn't dare ask her about it now though. A girl always appreciates the intention behind your pampering rather than the end result. It was another one of the million things that I loved about her. After finishing the coffee, she checked out of the hotel and we left in my car.

'Do you believe in the guru?' she asked, looking at me as I drove the car.

'You mean God?'

'Yes. This is a new start to our life together and I want to go to the gurdwara with you. Can we?' Jazz asked innocently.

'I'm not a hard-core believer, but for you, anything.' I smiled lovingly at her. And so, we went to one of the most famous gurdwaras in Mumbai at Four Bungalows.

'You know, the actual meaning of gurdwara is the residence of the guru, a spiritual guide who shows you the way from darkness to light,' Jazz explained.

Although I knew what she was talking about, I nodded in silence. I loved the way she innocently explained everything to me.

We removed our shoes at the *joota ghar* and, after covering our heads and washing our hands and feet, we entered the gurdwara to pay our respects to the Guru Granth Sahib.

'We consider the Guru Granth Sahib, the holy book, the eleventh guru, as the one who guides us spiritually. With a pure heart, you can wish for whatever you want.'

She made me close my eyes and wish for something but I had nothing to ask for. She was the one I wanted in my life and nothing else. Still, I asked for her happiness and good health.

Jazz closed her eyes and prayed, 'Babaji, you made me meet Aditya and I know you have shown me the right path always. I just hope that you continue to bless our relationship like you have always blessed me in times of need. I don't know what our future holds, but I have full faith in you and I'm sure you will guide us through our journey. I don't know how difficult it will be to convince my parents to accept this relationship, but I trust you. You have a solution for everything, so you must have a solution for my dilemma as well.'

I stood in awe of her while she prayed. I closed my eyes as she was about to open hers.

'Waheguru, I don't want anything but her happiness. I know she has prayed for our relationship, and I'm sure you won't break her trust.'

'Do you believe in the powers of *amrit*?' I asked her as we moved ahead and a person served us.

'Millions of people believe in it and so do I,' she said.

I respected her opinion and was glad she had brought me to the gurdwara. The vibe of the place was pleasing and positive, and it had a magnetic pull. I wasn't in the habit of sharing such personal feelings, but on the way back, I expressed the same to her, which somehow delighted her more. Though our religions were different, our souls were one; though our thoughts were different, our hearts beat for each other. The moment we confessed our love for each other, we wanted to be together forever, and although it had only been a few hours, it felt like we had shared more than months and years of togetherness. That's the power of.love!

For the first time ever, hours felt like weeks and seconds like days. Every minute that we were together, the world outside lost all importance and, for the first time, distance felt proportional to love. As we inched closer to the airport, I felt uneasy by the mere thought of separation. My prayers to God felt stronger and more powerful as I thought of the days ahead without her. After parking my car, we walked towards the departure terminal. Neither of us had said a word during the drive but my grip on her hand tightened. Jazz looked at me, teary-eyed. I felt torn. Her eyes begged me to not let go. The departure terminal gate was right in front of us, and there were people walking in all directions. She wrapped me in a tight hug as her tears started to fall.

'Don't cry,' I whispered softly. 'Whenever you think of me, I'll be there. Distance will never come between us. Our bond is stronger than it ever was; have faith in it.' I kissed her on the cheek.

'Please stop me from going. I don't want to leave you,' she said, still crying.

'You won't be away from me, dear. I will keep messaging you and calling. I love you. I'll wait patiently till I see you next, just to hold you and see you smile.' I tried to sound as convincing as I could, but, truth be told, I wasn't convinced either.

'I want to be with you, physically. If I miss you, I can't even hold your hand.' She had no intention of letting go and, in the middle of the crowd, we found ourselves, engulfed in love.

The overhead clock alerted us that it was time to say goodbye. Her crying had now turned to quiet sobs. I wished I could keep her with me forever, but she had to go. As she walked towards the departure gate, she looked back. The tears kept rolling, but this time it was I who was crying and she saw that. I could see that she wanted to comfort me but she was already late for her flight. Helplessly, she walked through the gate. The second she was out of sight, I messaged her.

Distance cannot separate our hearts as even though I am away from you right now, Jazz, I can still hear your heart beat in rhythm with mine. I smile to myself, thinking of the last few hours and days with you. Though we'll both be in different cities, our love will always make us feel like we are together. I miss you a lot already and I hope you feel the same. Appreciate this pain of love, for it will make us appreciate each other even more when we are together. Your love has strengthened my resolve to fight in difficult situations. I love you, Jazz, like no one can. You have given me the happiness that I longed for in such a short span of time. A simple thank you is not enough, but let me assure you, my love will never fade away.

Putting my mobile back into the pocket, I looked through the windows for one last glimpse of her. As I eventually walked back to the car, Jazz replied:

I already miss your warmth and your touch. You knew how to comfort me when I was with you and that is something no one else has ever done before. There are many things that I want to share with you, but there is no time to go through it all. I could spend my entire life telling you how much you mean to me and it still wouldn't be enough. You are everything to me and I want you to be my partner in crime. It's said everything happens for a reason and you came into my life to show me what true love is. I will fervently wait to be with you again. And when that time comes, you are not to leave my side for even a second. Promise?

I promised to be with her for as long as I was alive. Though she departed soon after for Delhi, she left her soul and heart with me in Mumbai. Long-distance relationships can be torturous; we desire to be with our loved ones through all the time that we spend apart. But togetherness and distance are just mere words if you have faith in each other and understand each other truly. Though we were separated by distance, the togetherness of our heart had the strength to defy all odds.

Farewell Hangover

So far, yet so close. What Jazz and I shared was nowhere close to a conventional relationship. We were dating but not like other couples who would meet daily; the only time we met was on Skype, on our laptop screens; we weren't like the couples who watched movies together in theatres, but we saw episodes of our favourite web series while chatting in another window. We didn't go on dinner dates to expensive restaurants every week, but we did share pictures and had dinner dates in the comfort of our own homes on video chat. We couldn't sleep in each other's arms, but we often fell asleep while still on the phone with each other. With each passing day, our relationship grew further and our trust for each other only strengthened. Sometimes we even had lonely nights fighting over the distance, which eventually ended with kissy-face emojis. Our friends laughed at us, calling us silly, but these were the favourite parts of our day—the times that we looked forward to the most. We would share fears, tears, smiles, laughs, frustrations and everything else; we had a point to prove—that long-distance relationships were not impossible. When you are with the right person, the distance only helps you become more mature as the emotional understanding that's required of you is unprecedented.

It was another such day and Jazz and I were on a video call.

'Why aren't you coming for Randeep's farewell party?' She made a sad face.

'If it was in my hands, I would. But I'm currently stuck with a few meetings here and Diwali is around the corner too. I have to be with my family.'

'Am I not your family?'

'You are, of course. Why would you say that?'

'Then why are you ignoring me? Fuck Skype, WhatsApp, Facebook, Twitter—I want you here right now.'

'I am not ignoring you. It's just that—'

'I am jealous of the people who get to see you every day,' Jazz continued.

Randeep was about to leave for the US and was throwing a farewell party for his close friends. Jazz, Priyanshi and Randeep wanted me to join them but it was practically impossible. Though Jazz tried convincing me, I was helpless. Work commitments were holding me back in Mumbai. However, I thought of a way to make her smile.

'Don't you remember your birthday is coming up? We will celebrate it together,' I said cheerfully.

'Where, on Skype? I want to be with you, *in person*!' she whined.

'It's your first birthday with me, we'll definitely make it special.'

'I know you won't.' She ended the Skype call abruptly and didn't answer my subsequent calls.

Sometimes distance makes things easier but, at times, it can make your life a living hell. If she was beside me, I could have made her understand my position easily but when you are miles apart you realize how dependent you are on technology, which, once taken away, leaves you vulnerable. She was not extremely furious, but a little upset due to my physical absence. Love makes you do crazy things in life, and I was next in queue. Though I knew that she would call me back after some time, I didn't want to take it for granted. After all, she was my priority, my soulmate.

I logged on to an e-greetings site and mailed her a few e-cards that had cute messages and graphics, one of which had her favourite teddy and an animated Minion. As she opened the greeting, the link asked her to enter her name to read a message from a loved one.

Jazz, she entered.

The message popped up with flying hearts on the screen.

The day you came into my life, you brought love along with you; a love too powerful to define. I'm sending you a heart to say I love you, Jazz. More than words can say!

She wasn't too surprised, since this was not the first time that something like this had happened. Over the next few days, for no reason other than to simply make her happy, I sent many such musical greetings. Along with them I sent her messages on WhatsApp.

Me: *It's been a while since we've met and hugged or looked into each other's eyes. We started as friends and it turned into a strong bond of love. I sometimes feel that the Fates are playing a prank on us to lord their dominance over us, giving us the joys and sorrows of a long-distance relationship. Whenever you call to say goodnight, I want to stop time and be with you in that moment for eternity. The hardest thing to do is stay away from you and love you but we will be together soon. I know it's difficult for you, just like it is for me, to be separated by miles, but true love knows no boundaries. Soon we will enjoy our togetherness like a festival of love. Just hold on till then, Jazz. Now go and enjoy the party. And miss me. *kisses**

Jazz had been sitting in her room, alone and dejected. But as soon as her phone beeped, she couldn't control herself and picked it up to read the message. As she read each line carefully, the sadness vanished and she felt pampered. Not wasting a second, she replied:

> Jazz: *I love you. I am sorry. I just get irritated sometimes without you. Will miss you at the party though.* ☹

Love as a feeling is very complicated, but if you have someone who understands you, the complications don't cause a hindrance when you try to reach out to that person you love. Jazz and I often had little arguments but we always found a way to resolve them because we were determined to make it work!

'Two vodkas, one whisky and . . . umm . . . what do you want to eat?' Randeep asked, turning to the two ladies, Priyanshi and Jazz.

'One chicken pizza and a pasta in red sauce. That's it for now,' Jazz said after checking with Priyanshi.

'Sure, madam,' the waiter said as he went to fetch their drinks.

Randeep's farewell party had kicked off at Smoke House Deli in Khan Market and though he was leaving India in a few days, their friendship was there to stay. For years now, they had lived together, laughed together and loved together. Randeep certainly was taking those memories of his crazy years with Priyanshi and Jazz with him. Tonight they would raise one last toast before he set out a new journey. The waiter served the food but the three of them continued drinking without paying any attention to it. They had seen all kinds of ups and downs in their friendship, but together they had withstood even the wildest storms. As Jazz was about to take the first bite of her pasta, she noticed something.

'What the fuck! There's a hair in my food. Call the waiter and ask him to throw this away. Yuck!' Jazz shrieked.

'It could just be yours, Jazz. The waiter doesn't have such long hair.' Randeep laughed.

'Their cook might be a lady.' She glared at Randeep, who only laughed harder.

'Just call the waiter,' Priyanshi said.

Randeep called the waiter who reached the table within seconds and when the matter was intimated to him, he looked perplexed.

'Do you want it replaced?' he asked.

'No . . . we don't want it. Take it away,' Priyanshi said aggressively.

'Call your manager,' Jazz raised her tone this time, which caused everyone else in the restaurant to look at their table.

'Sure, madam.' The waiter gave them a bright smile and went to find his manager and show him the pasta. The girls were already a few pegs down and more than just a little bit drunk by then. The manager spoke with the waiter before coming to their table.

'Don't worry, sir. We will replace the dish and you don't need to pay for it.' The manager spoke to Randeep.

'No . . . we don't want it,' Jazz answered.

'Then please tell us, ma'am, how may we make up for this inconvenience?'

'How about the waiter eats that portion in front of us?' Priyanshi, clearly drunk, grinned cheekily.

'Sorry?' The manager looked confused and the waiter cringed away in disgust at the mere thought of eating a hair.

'You heard it right. Tell him to eat that portion. We will pay,' Priyanshi clarified.

Before anyone could speak, Randeep apologized to the manager and the waiter for Priyanshi's behaviour. The restaurant staff left, taking the dish with them. Jazz couldn't stop laughing at what had happened.

'You should have seen his face.' Jazz giggled.

'Priyanshi has lost it.'

'Why? He wanted us to eat his hair, it's only fair for us to return the favour, right?' Priyanshi questioned, completely drunk.

For the rest of the night they laughed and joked and partied with the same fervour they had shared over the past few years. Randeep patiently tolerated both the girls as they continued to share memories of the humorous interactions they had shared in their long years of friendship. Even if they were going to be worlds apart, nothing, not even the oceans, could separate the love they had, the years of memories and happiness tying them together.

'What's wrong? Are you okay?' Randeep questioned Priyanshi.

'I'm fine,' she slurred.

Priyanshi was too drunk to walk. Randeep was holding her up so she wouldn't lose her balance. Jazz had left immediately after the party as she wanted to meet a colleague, leaving Randeep and Priyanshi alone. Randeep decided to drop Priyanshi home as she was too drunk to go back alone. They reached the parking lot where Randeep had parked his car.

'Get in,' he commanded.

'I want to drink more,' she pleaded.

Randeep ignored her incessant requests to drink more and started the car. Throughout the car ride, Priyanshi tried to convince him with her childish acts, telling him that she wanted to party some more with him as he was leaving her alone in India. But Randeep always knew when to stop. He continued to drive towards Dhaula Kuan.

'Please, I don't know when I will meet you again. Can't you do this much for me?'

'Don't worry. I will send you imported vodka bottles from the US.' Randeep smiled.

'You're so mean.' Priyanshi crossed her arms across her chest and groaned.

Randeep suddenly saw a flashing light in front. The light was at some distance but it certainly didn't look like the taillight of a car or any other vehicle, for that matter. He found it a little strange and eased off the accelerator. As they neared the source, the light turned out to be a big torch held by a man in the middle of the road.

Out of the blue, Randeep heard a loud noise. The impact of it was such that it scared him. Priyanshi regained her senses on hearing the sound and her high vanished into thin air.

Crack! The windows of the car cracked with a big bang. Four masked men with hockey sticks had attacked their car. It was scary! Randeep, although shocked and deeply afraid, didn't let it show, while Priyanshi shivered from the impact. Randeep didn't open the doors, neither did he speak a single word. The aggression in the men's eyes worried Randeep a little as he feared they would harm Priyanshi. Before Randeep could react, there was another fierce attack on the windows and the glass shattered. Gathering his courage, Randeep opened his door as there was no way he could move the car. Shards of glass pierced his neck and shoulders. As he got out, he told Priyanshi to stay inside.

'We want money. Give us whatever you have,' the men shouted in chorus.

'Who are you?' Randeep asked with authority, trembling with fear on the inside.

The next moment one of the men pulled out a knife and threatened to hurt Randeep, who immediately emptied his wallet to avoid the disaster that could easily ensue as he was with a girl. And then what he feared the most started to happen. Two of the men walked towards Priyanshi and threatened her with the knife till she emerged from the car.

'Look, I have given you the money. If you want my gold chain, take it. But don't mess with the girl,' Randeep pleaded.

'Is she a Nepali or a chinki?' one of the men commented as she came out of the car, trembling with fear.

'What's your name?'

'P-P-Priyanshi,' she stammered.

'Indian?'

'Yes. From Guwahati.'

On hearing this, they whispered amongst each other and then started inching closer to Priyanshi. She was horrified at what was happening.

One of them burst out, 'Do you people have no shame? Why do you even come to Delhi? Because of you chinkis, Delhi is a beggar today. You need to leave Delhi or leave the world right now. You have two minutes to decide.'

'Stop it or I will tell the cops,' Randeep screamed but the men held him tight so he could hardly make a move.

'Have you made your choice?' one of the men asked Priyanshi, pressing his knife to her cheek.

'Please leave me alone. I haven't hurt anyone. Please. I'm also an Indian,' she begged.

'No . . . no. You are a bloody chinki. Get out of here,' he yelled.

The men snatched all of Priyanshi's money, but before they could harm her any further, a police siren came to their rescue. Within seconds, the men fled away on their bikes. Randeep couldn't spot their number plates but once the cops reached the spot, he narrated the incident to them. They advised him to just leave though he wanted to file a complaint. None of the cops tried to make a note of the incident. The cops pretended as if nothing serious had really happened. Disappointed, Randeep drove Priyanshi home. Without exchanging a word, they walked into her apartment. Randeep brought her a glass of water for her from the kitchen and asked her to relax. However, the incident had shaken Priyanshi up pretty badly. The thug's words echoed repeatedly in her ears, traumatizing her to the extent where she just sat numb in front of Randeep, who was unsure of what he could say to make things better. He was also recovering from what had just happened, but he did so faster, seeing how Priyanshi was slowly slipping away. Though Randeep tried to comfort her, she was too caught up in what had just happened to them. Every word the men had said had been like a stab to her heart. It had been a very close shave. Priyanshi felt like she was running out of luck.

'I want to die,' she declared.

Randeep held her hand and sat beside her.

She continued talking. 'I want to die, did you hear me? I can't take it any more. It's over. Enough. I've had just enough.'

'What kind of loser says that?' Randeep was frustrated.

'Yes, I'm a loser. But I don't want to live any more. Please,' she continued.

'Listen to me. Sit quietly and listen.'

Furious and scared at the same time, Randeep had no idea what he was supposed to do. He had never seen Priyanshi like this. He hugged her in order to make her believe that everything was under control.

'Please stay with me. Without you, I am nothing. Jazz will be the only one left for me and you know that you must stick around for me! Please don't go.

'I want you to be strong. You aren't as weak as the things you're saying. I agree it was a disturbing experience, I'm still unsettled by it. Without any regard for my visa I was going to lodge a complaint, but what do you think would have happened? They would've harassed you more than the real culprits. Also, even if people talk shit, you know that you and every member of your family and the entire population of the North-east belongs to this country. These are uneducated people who go around talking shit. Being an intellectual, independent woman, you should take a strong stand rather than just give up on life. I may not always physically be there with you, but don't ever feel that I'm away from you. Be brave and live. Each time you step into your shell, people will try to take advantage of you and harm you. Now chill and give me a smile.'

Eventually, Priyanshi smiled. Randeep had helped her understand that there would be times when life would be really tough, but in such situations, it was imperative for her to be mentally strong. With every word from Randeep, her smile broadened.

'I'm sorry.' She hugged him.

For the time being, Randeep had managed to control the damage, but no one, least of all Randeep, knew how deeply the incident would affect Priyanshi.

Love > Distance

When you are in love, the happiness of your significant other becomes your priority and you strive to keep their smiles intact because nothing beats the satisfaction you get from seeing them happy, knowing the reason for that happiness is you. And although Jazz and I were like chalk and cheese, she always made an effort to make me smile; every time we argued, I made sure she didn't stay upset for too long. From the time our relationship took off, I realized that Jazz was extremely sensitive, which was sometimes difficult to handle. But isn't that the challenge that love brings with it? It was, after all, one of the many things that I loved about her. After Randeep's departure, she often felt lonely and missed their crazy weekends. Her birthday was around the corner, on 30 October, and she was convinced that this was going to be her worst one ever. Priyanshi had gone to Guwahati to meet her parents. Randeep was not in town either.

Jazz was upset and sent me a message on WhatsApp.

Jazz: *I am not going to celebrate my birthday this time as the people who mean everything to me are not here. Randeep, Priyanshi and you too. Even you are not coming.*

Me: *You aren't excited at all?*

Jazz: *Not even a little bit.*

Me: *Okay, help me buy your gift at least? Let's shop online for you!*

Jazz: *I just want you. That's it. I am so upset but you can't see it. Those gifts hold no value if you aren't the one handing them over to me. I need you here right now. You'd promised earlier that you'd make this birthday special. Are you turning back on that promise now?*

Me: *Are you angry?*

Jazz: *Does it even matter?*

Me: ☹

Jazz: *There's no point sending such useless smiley faces if you can't even show your face on my birthday. Bye.*

She didn't want to talk further as there was nothing left to say. She was yearning to hold on to something when there was nothing. We were together without being together and the distance from her friends added to her sadness.

> *I'm not sure whether you understand my frustration. If you don't, then I want you to. I dream about you being here with me in my arms and wishing me on my birthday, making it memorable. I can't express this directly, maybe I'm exaggerating a little, but I want you to understand how badly I miss you.*

She wrote out the message but immediately deleted it before dozing off.

The clock struck twelve and Jazz's phone beeped. I had sent her a birthday message as she didn't seem to want to respond to my calls.

> *Today is the big day. It's your birthday and I want to wish the most beautiful girl a very happy birthday. A single message from you brings a smile to my face. It's not as easy as it seemed to be, is it, this whole long-distance thing? It's sad that you are so far away, and time is taking its own sweet time to run its course. I wanted to celebrate this day with you but that seems impossible*

*now. Where could I find someone as adorable as you
who would love me the way you do? It breaks my heart
to be away, but even though we can't be together today,
I know you will have an amazing day. I love you, Jazz,
and it's your first birthday with me! I promise you won't
feel as if we are separated by distance at all.*

She replied with a mere 'Thank you. Goodnight.' Her
gloominess was evident in the text and she made it clear
that she wanted to be left alone.

When Jazz woke up early the next morning, her parents
wished her, after which they prayed together, but her face
wore a depressed expression. She faked a smile but her
eyes revealed her loneliness. She terribly missed her friends
and the love of her life. Behaving like it was any other day,
she pretended to be happy and left for work. Every time a
colleague wished her, it irritated her more and reminded her
of the void she felt inside her, a void that just kept growing.
Time passed, but nothing gave her contentment. She was
about to eat her lunch when she received a text message.
Sure that it was just another person wishing her a happy
birthday, she ignored it. But she couldn't bury the hope that
it was a name she wanted to see desperately. After trying
hard to restrain herself, she gave up and checked her phone.
It was a voice message. She quickly plugged in her earphones
to listen.

Aditya: *I know you want to kill me right now, and if you had a gun and a bullet, I wouldn't be spared. But as I said, it's your birthday and your first one with me. How could I not make it special? A day you would tell our kids about, how Daddy pampered Mommy. *kisses* Just give me a few hours. Today will be the best day of your life!*

Love makes you do crazy things, and when you are in a long-distance relationship, the craziness surpasses all limits. It's no less than a thrilling adventure which constantly engages your mind, your body and all your senses. I messaged Jazz and I was ready to blow her mind with the surprise that I had been planning for weeks.

'Welcome to Indira Gandhi International Airport. The temperature outside is 22 degrees Celsius. We hope you have a pleasant stay. Thank you for choosing Jet Airways.'

One more hour. I promise to bring a smile to your face. I messaged Jazz as I deboarded the plane and hailed a cab from outside the airport.

From the very beginning, I had pretended that I wouldn't be able to make it to Jazz's birthday. I wanted her to reach the nadir of her anger and then surprise her, so she wouldn't see it coming at all.

After listening to my message, Jazz probably expected me to send her e-greetings or love messages but there was more to it—and she had no clue about it. I wanted her to be surprised like never before. Surprise meetings make a relationship all the more special as they bring explosions of passion and love to life. All the longing that lasted for months would come to a close beautifully, months of longing compressed into those few moments shared together. Jazz was probably still at the office, upset, while I was already waiting outside. I messaged her once again:

Just a few more minutes. Your surprise will be in front of you.

The message made Jazz a little curious and she wondered what was going to happen next. I called one of her colleagues to make sure Jazz was at her desk on the top floor. I was thrilled just thinking about the fact that Jazz knew nothing about my plans. Her surprise was ready to unfold in front of her eyes! A local vendor had prepared the surprise, as instructed by me, and Jazz's colleague had collected it earlier that day. He had also bribed one of the security guards to deliver the huge and heavy package to the terrace of their office building. A few insiders had helped execute the entire plan, and once they reached the terrace and gave me the green signal, I called Jazz.

'Where are you?'

'What do you want?' She still sounded upset.

'Nothing. Just look outside your window in a few seconds,' I replied, staying on the line.

As instructed, she looked outside but saw nothing.

'There isn't anything there. I'm hanging up.'

'Now!' I exclaimed, as I saw the guard on the terrace execute the act.

The guard rolled down a huge banner which reached the third-floor window. It had the same text printed all over it with minimum spacing, which made it clearly visible from all the floors including the topmost. To people standing outside the building, it looked just like a plain white sheet. The guard gave me a thumbs up and held the banner still. The message read:

Happy birthday, my love, my lifeline, my soulmate. I love you, Jazz. You're mine forever.

As it was a glass building, the view was clear. The moment she saw it, her eyes welled up with tears of happiness. It was something no one had ever done for her and I was ecstatic at having fulfilled my promise of making her day memorable. It was a dream that she had always wanted fulfilled. She just stood there, stunned, till her colleague pinched her back to reality.

'Is this for real? You're unbelievable!' Suddenly the excitement in her voice was at its peak.

'You underestimated my love, my love,' I replied.

'Where are you?' Her voice became impatient.

'At the foot of your building.'

'What the fuck, really? Don't tell me you're serious!'

'Come down and see for yourself.'

'Shit, this can't be true. Am I dreaming?'

'You're in love.' I smiled.

She ran towards the lift and waited restlessly. I had a text ready for her and before she entered the lift, it was delivered to her.

I'm sorry for annoying you so much yesterday but I just wanted to surprise you and wanted to tell you that whenever I'm with you, your warmth gives me strength. You complete me, and trust me, I'm nothing without you. Your love and the love I have for you cannot be compared to anything. I am grateful that you have agreed to spend the rest of your life with me. I will do anything to make you the happiest person on earth. I want to redefine the meaning of love with you. I want to love you like no other man will and give you never-ending love. My day begins and ends with thoughts of you. Happy birthday once again. See you soon.

Within minutes, she was on the ground floor, looking at me, only a few feet separating us this time. Jazz was jumping in excitement. This was exactly what she had dreamt of the previous night and it was actually happening.

'You are one of the best things to happen to me. No one can ever replace you. Thank you so much for making me feel so loved and so important.' Jazz got emotional and hugged me.

A few jokes later, all of Jazz's anger from before evaporated. For the next few minutes, she didn't loosen her grip on my arms and repeated how much she loved and cared for me. Back at her cubicle, her colleague had bought a tiramisu cake, her favourite, on my suggestion. Her eyes twinkled when she saw it. After the birthday celebrations were over, she took her manager's permission to leave early. After thanking everyone, we left to spend our afternoon in the privacy of each other's company. She deserved all the love and pampering in the world and I intended to make sure she got it.

The passion we had for each other in our relationship made it perfect. Every time we met, it was no less than a celebration for us. Each time we met, I discovered a new side to her, and each time I fell in love a little bit more. Jazz was ecstatic to see me in Delhi on her birthday, which was my intention from the very beginning. To add to that, I decided to take her shopping for her birthday present to the Vasant Kunj malls. Like most girls, Jazz was crazy about shopping.

'Try this on.' I held up a pair of floral shorts while going through the women's section at Zara.

'No.' She grimaced.

'Then this one?' I picked another pair of shorts, hoping she would like it.

'Such hopeless choices, Aditya. Please let it be.' She made a face at me.

'So you mean you are a hopeless choice too, since you are also my choice?' I laughed.

'Nah, I'm the one good choice you made. You must have done something really good in a previous life to have found me,' she teased.

'Crap. Please continue shopping.'

After an hour of going through every store at the mall, Jazz finally found a dress she liked enough to buy; the whole affair was somewhat like going on a pilgrimage to all the holy shrines in the world. I was irritated, but I didn't dare show it, for it was her day.

'Let's look at something for you now,' Jazz declared, after I paid for the dress.

'No, I'm fine with what I have. Please.'

'Shut up. Look at yourself. You look like you're wearing your dad's T-shirt. You need some fashion advice, pronto!' Jazz commented and dragged me into Shoppers Stop.

143

'Wow, this will suit you so much,' she said, picking up a light peach shirt. 'You'll look like a superstar! Hold this.' She was beaming.

'I don't like—' I began.

Before I could complete my sentence, she admonished me. 'Did I ask you? Just try on whatever I choose. That's it.'

'You are looking at size forty; I wear a size forty-four . . . umm . . . okay, sounds like I'm a little overweight.' I blushed.

'A little? You should lose some weight. At least you should look good in your clothes,' she suggested.

'You want me to lose some weight right now? That's not possible.'

'You should start fitness training once you go back to Mumbai,' Jazz ordered as she pinched my belly playfully.

'By the way, I look great without any clothes on. Want to check?' I whispered, moving closer to her.

'Enough.'

Over the next five minutes, she selected more than half a dozen garments for me to try on, which irked me further. Focusing less on how they looked, I was trying to check the price tag to calculate the impact on my bank account.

'Baby, we've come here to shop for you, not me.' I tried to pamper her, but faltered at a fierce look from her.

When she chose a selection after scanning the entire men's section, I breathed a sigh of relief—but it was very short-lived. Unfortunately, Jazz loved everything she picked and, given no choice, my card was swiped.

'If I had known this, I would have stayed in Mumbai. Don't you think these are a little costly?' I winked.

'You are such a cheapskate.'

Jazz collected all the bags and walked out. Although the whole process of shopping with her had exhausted me and, to an extent, my bank balance, the only balance I cared about was the one we struck whenever we were together. When we sat down to eat at the food court, Jazz joked about how we had ended up shopping for me when we had actually come to buy stuff for her. Each minute with her so far had been very special. She had never missed an opportunity to tell me how much she had loved her surprise. She could have had anyone she wanted, but she had chosen me—and that made me feel all the more special. After lunch, we watched a movie, which was followed by a candlelit dinner—the perfect climax to her perfect birthday. Her words, not mine!

When I finally reached Mumbai, I had a new message from Jazz.

If 'I love you' was enough to express what I felt about you right now, I'd say it a thousand times over. You bring meaning to my life. I never imagined in my wildest dreams that someone would make my birthday so special and make me feel like a princess, until you came along. When we first hugged each other, our souls became one. Whenever I am with you, I'm carefree. I know there are better girlfriends than me in the world, but you truly are the world's best boyfriend. Thank you, and I love you. But don't forget, you must have done something really good to meet me. ☺

July 2015
Bandra

'Dude, are you serious? You wore a size forty-two? Like XXL?' Roma was surprised. Seeing me now, she couldn't believe I was once that big.

'Forty-four, actually,' I said, feeling embarrassed.

'You made a real effort to lose weight then!'

'I owe it all to Jazz, and Dipika witnessed it all.' I smiled.

'Oh yes, this idiot even stopped eating pizzas. He was so in love,' Dipika taunted.

'So you were his fitness guru?' Roma asked Jazz, who smiled in response.

'Not his guru. But inspiration maybe,' Jazz said, her smile making my stomach do a double flip.

She was right. If it wasn't for Jazz, I wouldn't have understood the importance of eating healthily and staying in shape. Although I was no hunk, I was no longer that overweight dork. At times, I would often get irritated by her constant nagging, but whenever she asked me to squeeze myself into a medium-sized shirt, I understood its worth. Not only that, her love made me a much more confident person.

'It would be rather accurate if I tagged her as my lucky charm. Lady Luck, as they call it.' I gave Jazz an affectionate smile, which she returned.

'Ooooh!' Roma and Dipika cooed together.

Love can either change you for the better or leave you with bitter memories. The extent of change or the intensity of bitterness varies with the depth of the connection you share. In my case, Jazz entered my life and changed me for the better, not only physically but emotionally and mentally as well, proving yet again that long-distance relationships work just fine.

'In fact, she was the one who forced me to grow this beard you see today, and after that I never dared to shave. I was afraid of change but her presence made it easier, and I saw the change in me soon enough.'

'Seriously?' Roma jumped up and down in her seat excitedly.

'Very.'

Jazz scrolled down my Facebook profile and showed her pictures from a few years ago, when I was fat and clean-shaven. Roma held the phone up next to my face and compared the old photos with reality.

'Jazz, you did a fine job with him!' Roma exclaimed, while Jazz blushed.

'Hey, I should be appreciated too. It's the person behind the beard who makes it look classy!'

'Oh please!' Dipika exclaimed.

'What?' I looked annoyed.

'I'm all for supporting Jazz on this one.' Dipika winked.

'Everyone knows who is classy here.' Jazz laughed mockingly.

Upset with the remarks, I finished my drink in one gulp and turned a blind eye to them all. Jazz took note of it, kissed my cheek and rested her head on my shoulder. She knew it made me melt every time she did that. The best part of our relationship was that we could persuade each other to do almost anything without having to say a word to each other. Jazz added spice to my life and kept the spark going. She will never know the extent to which she has made my dreams come true.

'Sir, we are taking last orders,' the manager notified us.

'Sure. Give us five minutes,' I said and asked for the menu.

As I studied the menu, Roma asked, 'Did Priyanshi ever recover from what happened that night?'

'Not really. In fact, after Randeep went to the US, she fell deeper into depression because of what had happened. She was scared to death every time she went out alone. Also, the UPSC results were going to be declared very soon. Though Jazz tried her best to keep Priyanshi happy, it gave her little solace, for she never really recovered.'

It was then that I realized how even a small incident can have a huge impact on your life. The scars you carry never completely heal, and they haunt you forever. Talking about Priyanshi's condition made us all step into a place so gloomy that it was hard for any of us to look each other in the eye.

'Your order?' The manager's presence brought us back to reality.

'One house special sizzler, one chicken biryani and one prawn biryani,' Dipika placed the order.

The manager nodded and left. Jazz was a little tipsy and wanted to use the washroom. After she excused herself, I followed her to make sure she was safe. I waited outside and from where I stood, I could see Dipika and Roma looking at me and saying something to each other. I just smiled and ignored them until Jazz came out.

'Let's click a few pictures over there,' Jazz insisted.

She grabbed my hand and dragged me into a corner of the restaurant to pose for selfies from different angles, with different facial expressions. We must have clicked at least a dozen selfies before she was completely satisfied. I somehow managed to look boring in each one, while she looked stunning. I was glad my phone memory was enough to save the zillion photos that she expected me to keep. Even if it was blurry and really bad, she wanted it saved. It was a little annoying but that's what made her happy, so I was happy too.

'I feel jealous. I still haven't found what you guys have. You people have raised my expectations now. You guys live hundreds of kilometres away, yet you never fight! I envy you so much. How can you be so unreal? Your kind of love story rarely exists,' Roma confessed when Jazz and I returned to our table.

I laughed. 'You're wrong, Roma. It is not that we don't have our share of fights and arguments. So far we have been in the honeymoon phase of our relationship.'

'You mean . . .'

'Yes. Long-distance relationships are indeed every bit as difficult as they say they are.'

'I don't believe it. What would you two even fight about?'

'Do you need reasons? A simple statement can sometimes make headlines.' I winked at Jazz to let her know that I was only kidding.

As the waiter served us our food, I continued with the story.

Dear Heart, Please Stay
in Your Limits

There is always a looming uncertainty that overshadows all relationships, and ours was no exception. Jazz and I, we had our ups and downs too. Our life was not a fairy tale with the perfect set-up, the perfect love story, ending in a happily ever after. After the initial honeymoon phase, we too had arguments, sometimes for no particular reason. More often than not, we avoided communicating and clamped down on our feelings, pointing fingers at each other, which aggravated the situation further instead of diffusing it. Long-distance relationships are plagued by the usual problems, with the added factor of distance. But I realized that besides all that, the real challenge lay in the mental conflicts that occurred when there was no intersection between expectations and reality. While I preferred texting, she liked talking on the phone better. When we interacted without video calls, we weren't able to see each other's expressions, which led to misunderstandings in comprehending the tone of a text. Though I had completed my management studies, I sucked when it came to managing my own time and schedule, which is why most of my plans were made at the last minute and this often led to disputes. At the beginning of the New Year, Jazz's work timings changed and her late-night shifts brought further chaos to our relationship.

'I am simply fed up with your inhuman work timings, Jazz. When I want to discuss something you are sleeping and when normal human beings are asleep, you want to discuss the most important issues in the world.'

Half asleep, I was on a call with Jazz at three in the morning. I had already retired for the day, but she wanted to discuss her work problems.

'You know very well, Aditya, that my brother is back only for a few days. My parents and I spend all the time we can get with him because he only comes home once every year. Is this so hard to understand or you are too immature to understand my point of view?' Jazz shouted in frustration.

'I understand, but that doesn't mean that all our conversations have to take place at this hour of the night. Can't you just leave your house for some time during the day so you can call me?'

After a tiring day, it was sometimes impossible to stay awake till the wee hours of the morning, though it was a regular thing for Jazz. And to make the bad timing worse, Jazz's elder brother, Bon, was visiting from the US, where, after completing his education, he had stayed on to work. He was quite possessive about her and, like any other brother in the world, cared for her more than anything. Her happiness meant everything to him and he never tolerated tears in her eyes. He pampered her even more than her parents did! Due to his overprotectiveness, Jazz hadn't told Bon about our relationship, as she wasn't sure how he would react, which is why she became even more cautious at home and ignored my calls until she left home for work. It would be an understatement to say that the last few days had been maddening.

'No, I can't. And you know exactly why. The same person who used to stay up until dawn to talk to me in the initial days of our relationship now thinks that it's all crap. Wow. I think it's best if we stopped talking; at least that way I won't share anything with you. You haven't even noticed that over the last few days, I have avoided discussing important things with you.' Jazz reacted, her voice heavy with disappointment.

'I am not saying that I'm not up for a conversation, I am. But every day? At this ungodly hour? Isn't that too much to ask for? Sometimes you could also adjust to my schedule, right? And I'm not feeling well either.' I tried to reason with her.

'Okay, fine then.'

'Now what?' I asked.

'Nothing. Bye. Goodnight. I hope you get a good night's sleep after having royally pissed me off.'

'Don't start again, please . . . Did I . . .'

Before I could persuade her, she cut the call abruptly and also blocked me on WhatsApp. Although it was temporary, she did it for her peace of mind, after having completely messed with mine. Trying to navigate a long-distance relationship is a task next to the impossible!

That night she went to work thinking, 'Why is he behaving so weirdly?' and in another city, my last thought before falling into the comfort of sleep was, 'We used to love each other like crazy. What went wrong?' We hadn't had the luxury of hugging, kissing or holding hands and looking into each other's eyes for a very long time, which was probably why tensions were running so high between us and why we were so stressed all the time. Our love hadn't deteriorated, but, for a long time, these petty misunderstandings prevailed, blinding us from the love we had for each other.

The next morning, the fight continued. While I slept, the intensity of her anger grew. I only realized to what extent when I found out that she had blocked me from Facebook too, leaving no alternative to contact her except through normal text messages, to which she didn't reply. Where social media had made life easier, it had also made relationships more complicated. With no option left, I sent her a text.

Let's end last night's argument, please? It's a new day and it brings new hope; let's not start the day by feeling miserable about yesterday's troubles. Can't we smile and love each other instead of wasting our time and energy on stupid fights? Please forgive me and unblock me. I am sorry if I hurt you. Sexiness lies in forgiveness. So let's be sexy together. ☺

I stared at my phone for a while, waiting for her reply, but she preferred to ignore me. Again. Who was I kidding?

Dipika and I had made plans the previous week to meet for lunch that afternoon, but after the fight I was a little unsure about whether I wanted to go out at all. However, blowing off Dipika at the very last minute would have been inappropriate. Thus, I decided to suck it up and meet her for lunch.

'How's Jazz?' she asked me as we sat in the car.

'Currently blocked.' I smiled.

'You blocked her? What the . . .' Dipika looked shocked.

'Me? Block her? Do you think I have the guts?' I laughed and continued, 'We had a small argument last night and . . .'

Before I knew it, I was telling Dipika all about our fight from the night before, and the night before that, and the one before that . . . well, you get the gist. We continued to talk about it and Dipika advised me to be patient with her and calmly make her understand the situation, something I had tried before, and failed miserably at. After waiting for half an hour, we finally got a table for two at Irish House Cafe in Lower Parel. While we waited for our drink orders to arrive, Dipika clicked a picture of us and uploaded it to Facebook, tagging me in it.

Little did I know that this would later land me in more trouble with Jazz. How on the earth was I supposed to assume that even though she had blocked me, she was still keeping an eye on my profile. The moment she saw the tagged photo, she unblocked me in order to send me over twenty WhatsApp messages to show her annoyance, only to block me again before I could even reply.

I so hate this game of blocking and unblocking, I thought as I read through more than a dozen WTFs in under a minute.

I excused myself from the table, and Dipika could tell from the solemn look on my face that I was trying to call Jazz. Fortunately, Jazz answered on the first ring.

'Why have you called me? Go enjoy yourself with your friends, Aditya. Anyway you don't care whether I cry or die,' Jazz hissed.

'Why are you saying all this? I just called to clear the air. Let's please clear the air, Jazz,' I begged.

'I think it's too late to clear the air now. I don't want to even talk to you. Instead of just calling me once, you're happily partying there. You've made my life a living hell.'

Losing my patience, I said sternly, 'I called you so many times. I even texted you. And I'm not partying, I just came out for lunch with Dipika. She's your friend too!'

'Whatever. Just get lost. You have made a mockery of my life. I don't want to talk to you any more, bye.'

Without giving me a chance to explain, Jazz disconnected the call. What she didn't realize was that Bon had heard everything she'd said from outside her room. When he came inside, Jazz knew she was in trouble. Though she pretended to act casually her fear soon caught up with her—the fear of being caught by her brother. Her heart pumped faster and she wished fervently that he hadn't heard the entire conversation.

'Who was that? Are you dating someone?' Bon asked with a serious expression on his face, as he sat down on a chair next to Jazz's bed.

His eyes ignited fear in her heart. Somehow, she mustered up the courage to lie and denied his accusation. However, Bon didn't seem too convinced by her obvious fib.

'You can't get away with lying to me, Jazz. I'm you're elder brother after all and I wasn't born yesterday, so I know exactly what's going on. At least be true to yourself.'

'No, Bhaiya. I'm . . .' Jazz stammered.

'I'm asking you for the final time, Jazz, before I take the next step,' Bon threatened.

He continued to nag Jazz until she finally gave in. She told him everything, from the very beginning, keeping no secrets from him this time. She even told him about her ongoing fight with me, which angered Bon beyond comprehension. He was shocked and disappointed at how Jazz could trust someone she met online and date him. Bon found it hard to believe that they truly shared genuine feelings for each other despite her incessant attempts to convince him otherwise.

'I don't want to hear another word. It is all crystal clear to me now. The guy just wants to use you. He just wants fun. You're a smart girl, Jazz. You should stay away from such freaks. How could you fall for such a trap? This is so common back in the US and it always ends badly. You're my little sister and I must protect you from wandering on to the wrong path.'

'But, Bhai . . .' Jazz protested.

'You're arguing with me, your elder brother, who's known you all your life, for that freak, whom you met four days ago? I care for you and want you to stay away from all these things, or you'll end up hurting yourself. Consider it a warning or brotherly advice, but I hope you won't break my trust and make me take a drastic step. Right?'

'Why don't you try to . . .?'

'Right?' Bon repeated, and something in his tone told Jazz that he wasn't going to take no for an answer.

'Okay, Bhai,' Jazz muttered, dejectedly.

Jazz had always looked up to him. He had always been her guide and confidante, which is why she was even more heartbroken with his decision. He was the one closest to her and she worshipped him. She wanted to choose love but, at the same time, she didn't want to go against her brother's decision and betray his trust. Though she did try, Bon was in no mood to change his mind anytime soon.

How will I break the news to Aditya that Bon is not ready to accept our relationship and I can't go against his wishes? Rather, I don't want to go against his wishes because of everything that he has done for me since childhood. Not only as a brother but as a friend, he's always been my safety net. The hardest thing I've ever had to do is to let go of you. I doubt if my heart will ever love after this tragedy. From the moment we met, I haven't been able to imagine my future without you. The dreams we shared, the hopes we had for the future, is it all over? Aditya, I still love you. Do you believe me, especially after the way I reacted last night and again this morning?

Jazz's thoughts kept jumping from me to the promise she had made to Bon. She realized that no matter what she did, no matter how hard she tried, the end was near. The end of what though, she wasn't sure. On one hand, there was Aditya, whom she loved like there was no tomorrow and, on the other hand, there was Bon, her brother, her blood. No matter what happened, she also knew that the love she felt for Aditya would never diminish, not even with time. She would forever carry it in her heart.

Her phone rang; Aditya was calling. She didn't pick up. He called again.

Despite receiving multiple calls from me, she answered none for she had decided to ignore them. It wasn't clear to anyone what was going on in her mind, but, at that moment, she decided to put an end to everything. She wrote out a text the next moment:

Please don't disturb me. I just don't want to be further involved in this mess that we're in because of your lies. You stay with your friends forever and I'll stay with mine. Let me live my life. I just can't take it any more. It's over for me and that's my final decision, so don't even try to come back to convince me otherwise. You might think I'm being rude, but that's what you deserve. And the truth is you don't deserve someone like me.

Tears, lies, goodbyes, no hugs, no kisses, lonely nights and long fights, and the promise made to Bon—it had all led up to this drastic step, breaking not one but two hearts at once.

More than anyone else, it's often life that plays with our feelings in the most brutal ways, keeping us shackled to misery with no escape. Jazz's message froze all my senses, and for a minute, I thought she was joking. Hoping I was right, I called her immediately and asked, 'Is this a prank?'

'No, I'm serious, Aditya; please don't call me again and again. I am with my family and I've made my decision,' she replied coldly.

Without giving me a reason, she ended the conversation abruptly, the silence at the other end indicated the end of my life as well. Jazz had come to me after months of convincing and pleading, but it only took her seconds to extinguish that togetherness. I still couldn't wrap my head around this reality, but, like a bitter pill, I had to digest this as well. However, it was not as simple as deleting a number from your phone book or blocking a person on Facebook. She had been imprinted on my soul for a lifetime and I take the vows I make very seriously. I lost count of the calls I made or the messages I sent her over the next few hours, completely disregarding the fact that she had asked me to stay away, but from where I stood, I could see no hope of us getting back together. In that moment, I knew I was alive, but I felt dead inside. Painfully, I remembered and revisited every word had she said, each cutting my heart like a knife. She conveniently blamed it all on me and how we hadn't been getting along as smoothly over the last few days without even trying to sort things out. I might as well have dug a grave and watched her fill it up as I lay there at the bottom, still with hope in my heart that she would stop and help me out instead, wanting me in her life once again. She was the one who taught me how to fly but she was also the one who pushed me over the edge, knowing I was afraid of heights, deliberately not being there to catch me as I fell.

'What happened?' Dipika asked.

'I'm clueless. I'm sure she didn't end this relationship because of a stupid tag on Facebook . . . did she?' I was devastated.

'Obviously not. But you should have at least asked her the real reason for all this. You both love each other, right?'

'I know I do. I did try asking her, but she wouldn't answer.'

'Shut the fuck up. She loves you too and you know that.'

'Then what's the issue here? Why did she take such a drastic step?' I whimpered, the hurt in my voice evident.

'You need to clear it out, dude. It can't go on like this.' Dipika sighed.

Dipika anxiously dialled Jazz's number from her phone to find out the truth, once and for all. However, Jazz ignored her calls too. Dipika even left messages asking her to call, but all in vain. I could sense a familiar lump rising in my throat. I'd done everything right; I'd done everything for her. And yet, it took her only a few seconds to forget about all of that and discard me like a used tissue. I thought our love was stronger than this, stronger than a little fight about scheduling, but I'd been mistaken. I'd been mistaken about a lot of things. After I reached home, I left her another frantic and desperate message.

I don't know whether you'll even read this message, but I wanted you to know a few things. I promise to never lie to you, and always be true to you; to always lend you a shoulder to lean on and listen when you need to share your doubts and worries; to hold you when you need someone, to always care for you, and to be there whenever you feel alone. I also promise to never hurt you and break your heart, to always lift you up when you are down, to wipe your tears when you feel like crying, to keep you smiling in that alluring way that you do. Jazz, I will always love you, more than anything else, until the end of time. Please forgive me and come back to me. My life is a meaningless abyss without you. I know there is something more to this decision of yours but together we will resolve it and overcome all obstacles. Just one chance, that's all I want. Maybe I'm not worth it right now, but I promise I will be.

Jazz saw the message pop up on her screen and went back into her room, avoiding her brother. After reading the message, she texted back:

Aditya, it would be good if you too accept that we can't be together. We are very different from each other. People say that they will always be there for each other, but is that truly so? A long silence will follow but our love won't grow. They say that time will bring us love but I think otherwise. Acceptance will grow but not love. I have realized that in a relationship, only the initial days can give you all the happiness and love, later it's just an addiction or obsession, whatever you call it, with the person—the need to make an attachment that forces one to stay. But I just can't be your addiction, Aditya. You chose to ignore me before and now I've made up my mind to kill this addiction that you presumed to be love.

Jazz couldn't help but let a few tears escape as she finished writing the message. If only she could tell Aditya the real reason behind her coldness, but she had made a promise to Bon, and she intended to keep it. She sent the message and put on a fake smile before entering the living room; Bon looked at her puffy eyes suspiciously, but said nothing.

Love, for us, is an illusion. The only constant love I ever had is to forever be in love with the idea of love. Perhaps, the hardest unspoken setback of any break-up is when you have all these beautiful memories with your significant other, but you have no idea what to do with them. I felt a massive void taking form within me. For years, everyone asked me how I could craft stories about successful relationships with such ease and I would only smile and brush the question aside politely. Little did they know that I craved the kind of love that I wrote about and, with Jazz, I had thought my search was over but reality had proven my desires wrong more than once.

Life's Rude but I'm a Dude

'Don't you think you've ended everything too abruptly? You should give yourself and this relationship a little time, Jazz. I'm sure Bon will understand how serious you are about Aditya once he sees the depth of your feelings for him,' Priyanshi advised.

'I can't argue with Bon, you know that. I respect him more than anything, and arguing with him would be insulting his decision. He has taken care of me my entire life. How can I just betray the trust he has had in me all these years?' Jazz sobbed.

'I am not asking you to go against his decision but at least try to convince him. You might regret not doing so later.'

'You think I haven't done that?' Jazz reacted.

'But you love Aditya,' Priyanshi stated matter-of-factly.

'I love Bhaiya too, and right now, I'm just doing what I think is correct.'

'Will you be able to stay away from Aditya?' Priyanshi looked worried.

'Of course not. I'm madly in love with him. But all I'm saying is that right now, I can't argue with my brother. In a few days, I will try again to make Bhaiya understand how important Aditya is to me. But till then, I need to close this chapter.' Jazz wanted to change the subject and suddenly remembered Priyanshi's results were due. 'Aren't your results out tomorrow?'

'That's what everyone is saying. I don't know how I will face my parents if I flunk,' Priyanshi said, dejected.

'Don't be negative. I'm sure you will clear the exam and make your parents proud.'

While Jazz was heartbroken about her own situation, an air of nervousness and melancholy surrounded Priyanshi. They were too depressed to lift each other's spirits. A sinking feeling engulfed Priyanshi but she knew she had to struggle through this phase as well. Heartbreak had destroyed Jazz but it was up to her now to patch her heart up.

'Give her some space. She's probably disturbed about something else,' Dipika stated.

'But why is she hiding it from me? What have I done? We used to be friends, but now I don't know if we still are,' I said.

Life felt like it was in reverse gear, my loss seemed irrecoverable and all hope for the future was forever lost. I was standing on the pavement with Dipika, sharing with her my grief. I couldn't think straight and nothing made sense to me. We stood there trying to fathom why Jazz was acting the way she was, but nothing reasonable came to mind. *How am I to cope with this?* I asked myself as my heart felt like it would explode into a million pieces, taking me down with it.

And then, before I knew it, there was a loud clang and I was on the ground. Before Dipika could react or even warn me, the weight of misfortune, which in reality was an iron pole, had fallen on me, and I lay flat on the road, my legs throbbing in pain. For the next few minutes, I tried to understand what was happening. All I could feel was excruciating pain. My back screamed in protest and I felt like someone was choking me. I could see a crowd gathering around me, while a few people splashed what felt like water on my face. I tried to resist the pain, but my body wouldn't obey. Straining my eyes, I tried to focus and find a familiar face, till my eyes rested on Dipika. I could see blood starting to pool around me but I didn't know its source. I tried avoiding the blood, which seemed to be flowing towards me, but my body wouldn't oblige at all. My head felt like it would explode.

'Are you okay?' Dipika sprinkled something wet on my face.

'I'm dying,' I replied.

'Call an ambulance! Fast! Please, it's a request,' Dipika pleaded to the crowd.

'I'm dying,' I repeated, my eyelids starting to feel heavy.

I could hear the crowd shouting around me but I couldn't comprehend what they were saying. I tried to sit up but my body betrayed me for the third time. My legs felt uncomfortable but I couldn't move them, and when I finally brought myself to focus on them after blinking several times, I saw a huge electric pole resting on top of my knees. Somehow, I felt no pain in my legs; in fact, I couldn't feel them at all. Perhaps, they were paralysed. That's when realization hit me. An electric pole had fallen on me. There were bruises all over my body. I could feel myself slipping slowly, but there was one thing I needed to do before my body gave up on me completely. I brought out my phone from my pocket with extreme effort and dialled the first number on speed dial. No one picked up. I tried again, knowing this would be my last attempt. I heard the phone ringing and, this time, she answered.

'Now what's wrong with you? Didn't I ask you to stay away? Yet you disturb me every hour. I will block you for a lifetime, Aditya!' Jazz shouted from the other end.

I choked out the words, 'I am dying.'

That's all I could say. I didn't have the strength to speak any more. Jazz must have thought that it was a prank but when I tried to explain that it wasn't, all that came out of my mouth were grunts. That's when she realized that I hadn't been joking and started to panic.

'What? How? Where are you? Who is with you?' she asked frantically.

However, before I could answer the phone slipped from my hand and I drifted into unconsciousness. Tick-tock . . . tick-tock . . . I felt like life had begun its final countdown. My memories flashed, one after the other, before my eyes. Most of them included Jazz. I wished I could turn back time and spend it with loved ones and cherish what was once within my reach, but was now so far away.

Dipika informed my parents, who rushed to the hospital where the ambulance had taken me. They were a mess. Dad, a lively person by nature, feared losing his only son and Mom, like all overprotective mothers, broke down the moment she saw me in the hospital bed.

The doctors, after examining the X-rays, declared, 'We need to operate on his leg. There is internal bleeding. But we need to wait till his blood pressure comes to normal.

Until then, he needs to be on oxygen.' My mother started crying on Dad's shoulder the moment she heard the word 'operate' and my father coughed to hide a sob.

Dipika was the only one who had the strength to speak. 'For how long do we have to wait before he is operated on? Will he be fine? It's not too serious, right?'

'We'll operate after twelve hours, if things go well. I won't say it's not serious, but such cases are successfully dealt with in most cases,' the doctor reassured everyone.

Jazz was with Priyanshi in her room when she received the call. After she hung up, Jazz felt like a bus had hit her, as if her body, soul, mind and heart had been completely destroyed. She wanted to scream out loud, but she couldn't make a sound. She sat there, numb, feeling nothing but emptiness.

She thought to herself, *I broke your heart, Aditya, and you didn't even know why. I refused to tell you because I was afraid you wouldn't understand my perspective. I still love you but you hurt me too. I know you did this on purpose so that I wouldn't fight with you. You are selfish. How could you think of only yourself and leave me alone? Why did you do this to me? I was not going anywhere, and you decided to quit life before it was your time? I was a part of your life too! Didn't you always say I was your life? Then how could you decide to kill me without my permission? I am not ready to die. I, your life, want to breathe and laugh and sing and dance with you!*

'Jazz . . . Jazz!' Priyanshi shook Jazz by her shoulders, but she just sat lifeless, still as a statue.

When she finally looked into Priyanshi's eyes, she burst into tears. She wailed so loudly that the neighbours heard her and came to check if everything was all right. Priyanshi was stunned to see the way Jazz cried her heart out.

Assuring the neighbours that everything was okay, she addressed Jazz. 'What's wrong?'

'Aditya . . .'

Priyanshi's heart sank. 'Aditya? Is he okay?'

Jazz kept repeating his name, but said nothing else. Priyanshi was extremely scared and Jazz's sadness made her heart heavy. After insisting and shouting and shaking her back to reality, Priyanshi was able to make Jazz reveal what she knew about the incident. Priyanshi called Dipika immediately.

'How is Aditya?' Priyanshi asked in a rushed manner, skipping the conventional pleasantries.

'We are at the hospital. He is unconscious. His parents are here. I will talk to you later,' Dipika said hurriedly.

'Please, Dipika, tell me, what's the situation? Jazz is uncontrollable, she's with me,' Priyanshi pleaded.

Dipika asked Priyanshi to hand the phone over to Jazz. Terrified, Jazz didn't take the phone at first but fear for Aditya's well-being got the better of her. She brought the phone to her ear.

'Jazz, are you listening?' Dipika asked.

'Yes,' Jazz said.

'Come here as soon as possible. Tonight, if possible, or early tomorrow. Please. He's not good,' Dipika said and hung up.

Jazz immediately opened her Goibibo app only to close it the next minute. Her conscience reminded her of the promise she had made to Bon, her brother. But the last words Aditya had said to her came rushing back and she felt ashamed. She wiped her tears and walked out of the room.

'Where are you going?' Priyanshi asked.

'To talk with Bhai,' Jazz said with conviction.

Slamming the door behind her, her inner voice awakened, she decided to follow her heart, going against her brother's verdict of separation.

Jazz reached home, and on seeing Bon alone, she told him everything and pleaded with him to let her go to Mumbai. Bon remained silent throughout, and Jazz took it as an opportunity to convince him further.

'I will do whatever you say after this but, just this once, let me go. He needs me and he's in a critical condition.

Please don't be so rigid. I know you care for me, but, trust me, I'm not wrong.'

'What if he is lying?' Bon shook his head.

'No, he isn't. How can I make you believe me? He is not fake, Bhaiya.'

Jazz understood that Bon was not wrong to be suspicious. Being a guy, he knew how men thought. He also knew that some online relationships do work, but he was just trying to protect his sister. Which brother would let his sister fall for a cheat? But when Jazz poured her heart out in front of him in a long and detailed discussion, he saw the intensity of her love and care and the high regard she had for her love. Seeing her cry, his heart melted.

Finally, Bon replied, 'Does he love you like you love him? I know you think I'm trying to be the villain here but I have my reasons too, Jazz. However, I can't see you crying, and no one should ever make you cry, not even me. You are my pride and I just want only happiness for you. I was unhappy and suspicious when you first told me about him, but if your happiness lies with him, then so does mine.'

Jazz couldn't control her tears any longer; she embraced Bon and thanked him for understanding her so well. Keeping their sisters happy, isn't that what brothers are for? Bon had gone over my Facebook profile to see if I was the same guy of whom his sister had spoken so highly. Jazz could always count on him as he had always been her pillar of strength, which was why he also decided to accompany her to Mumbai. He was the best brother she could have asked for. At that moment, Jazz felt everyone should have a brother like hers so they would have someone to protect them like a father, care for them like a mother and give them the companionship of a friend.

The next morning, Bon and Jazz departed for Mumbai, without disclosing to their parents the real reason for their visit. Before leaving, Jazz informed Priyanshi, who comforted her by saying that everything would be fine and under control very soon. They prayed together silently before parting. The journey was only a couple of hours long, but it felt like an eternity to Jazz. She felt like she had aged ten years overnight, but she was thankful for Bon's support. His presence gave her strength and helped her stay composed, especially when she thought she would fall apart. She remembered everything we had shared over the past couple of months, from the late-night calls, sometimes just to ask if she had reached home on time, to every little fight we had, fights that seemed so irrelevant and small to her now. She remembered what it was like to hug me. How, sometimes, I would adore every last bit of her and tell her she was irresistible. Different thoughts and images, from the times we had spent together, played in her mind as the flight landed in Mumbai. Even in the cab on the way to the hospital, she kept herself composed, thinking about the funny manner in which I ate, till she saw Dipika and collapsed into in her arms.

Dipika took her by the hand and led her towards the room.

'How is he?'

'Still unconscious. The doctors are going to operate in an hour.'

Jazz saw my family sitting in the lobby, but didn't speak to them immediately out of fear. When my parents left to complete some hospital formalities before the operation, she caught a glimpse of me. Her heart sank and, for the second time in twenty-four hours, she felt like she'd been hit by a bus. Her stomach lurched and she thought she might be sick. Seeing me with an oxygen mask and in a hospital gown, wires connecting me to machines beeping softly in the background, she couldn't stop her tears. She felt like she was choking and drowning at the same time. She came closer to me and ran her fingers through my hair, hoping that I would wake up and smile at her mischievously, like nothing had changed. But nothing of the sort happened.

'Excuse me.'

Jazz saw a team of doctors entering the room along with my parents and jumped away from me immediately.

177

Dipika introduced her to my parents as my friend but they were not in any state to greet her. Jazz didn't mind at all, for she knew exactly what they were going through. Everyone's eyes were glued to the doctor inspecting me. The nurses and the ward boy requested everyone to leave the room, as they were about to shift me to the operation room.

After transferring me from the bed to a stretcher, they moved towards the operation theatre and everyone followed them with heavy hearts. When the doors to the operation theatre closed, my parents, Jazz, Dipika and everyone else present became nervous and scared. The next three hours made everyone realize how difficult it is to see your loved ones hurt. After the surgery, the doctors came out and informed them that they had to insert a plate in my leg to fix the bones and that there were no major spinal injuries. Fortunately, the electric pole had knocked me unconscious, leaving me immobile, thus preserving my spine.

'He is fine. But he's still under anaesthesia. He should regain consciousness in an hour or so.' The doctors smiled.

Everyone let out a collective sigh of relief. Once the nurses shifted me to the room, it was only a matter of time before I woke up. Right on schedule, I opened my eyes to a room full of my loved ones, anxiously waiting for me to wake up. I looked at my parents and said, 'Mom, Dad . . . I want to go home.'

Dad became emotional and Mom rushed to my side, holding my hand tightly.

'Nothing happened to you, right? You're okay?' I asked Dipika, remembering she had been there with me when it had happened. She nodded, and I said, 'If only you had kicked my ass that time, the pole would have fallen on the road and not me.' I tried to smile.

'Shut up,' Dipika said, turning red.

Finally, my eyes rested on Jazz, who had been standing in a corner of the room all this time. For the first few seconds I thought I was hallucinating because of the painkillers, but when she came closer and sat next to me, I realized that she was actually there. When my parents left to get something from the cafeteria, Dipika was outside talking to Priyanshi on the phone and Bon was in the waiting room, I asked Jazz to come close and I softly whispered in her ear, 'Please don't leave me again. I love you.'

Trying her best not to cry, she assured me, 'I love you more than you love me. Never do this to me again.'

I started to feel drowsy but insisted on staying awake. The nurse stepped in finally. 'Let the patient rest. Don't disturb him too much right now, he needs to sleep. Tomorrow, he'll feel a lot better.'

While Dipika had to leave for the day, Jazz and Bon, along with my parents, decided to stay back. Bon made Jazz eat despite her resistance as he didn't want her compromising on her health and adding to everyone's problems. Calmly, he fed her and made her drink juice but she couldn't sleep the entire night despite Bon's protestations. She had switched off her phone to avoid any disturbances, but even then, sleep evaded her. In the morning, after the nurse gave me breakfast, my dad went home to bring a change of clothes and Mom went to buy my medicines from the store. Jazz and I were alone again.

'I am sorry. But this is not the way to punish someone. You know how scared I am of doctors and hospitals. But you still did this. Please let's go home.' Jazz began crying.

'Don't cry. I'm feeling so much better now. The leg will take time to heal, but, otherwise, I'm the same as I was, Jazz!' I tried taking off the covers to show her but she refused as she was scared and couldn't see me in that condition any longer.

Kissing my forehead and holding my hands, she gave me a letter she had written.

You think you're the only one who can write. I can too, although I never thought I would write for the first time sitting outside your hospital room. The girl who couldn't stay away from her phone and Facebook— you made her forget that phones exist. From the time I reached here, I have not once checked my phone. I *have just been praying for your recovery. Each time I hear you're not well, my eyes well up. The demons in my heart paralyse me and I start to think I could never smile until you do. The happiness in my life suddenly eroded away, caught in the eye of a tornado, when I saw you in your bed, connected to all those scary looking machines, tubes sticking out of your arms and chest. In the last few hours, life has been a whirlwind. It will continue being this way till you get up and take me for a long drive, or just hold my hand and kiss me. Don't make me wait too long. I promise that as long as I am with you, no one can even touch you. I love you; just please don't punish me this way again. Do whatever you want, but if you do it again, I will hurt myself too and then you will realize how it feels. I am yours and yours only. Just get better soon and then take me on a holiday. *kisses**

I pulled her close and kissed her forehead when she bent to wrap her arms around me.

'I am sorry. And I love you.'

Our embrace was interrupted by Bon, who entered the room just then and exclaimed, 'Please take care, buddy. There are so many people wishing for your recovery. Get well soon.' I thanked him for allowing Jazz to come to Mumbai.

The road to recovery is always a bitch. The doctors had ordered bed rest for a few weeks. They didn't declare a discharge date, but when Bon saw that my condition was improving, he decided that it was time for him and Jazz to fly back to Delhi to avoid complications at home. Though Jazz didn't want to leave me alone for a minute, she knew she had to go back. After booking a late-evening flight, Bon promised me that Jazz would return as soon as I was discharged from the hospital. Before leaving, Jazz and I looked at each other one last time. The love and affection we had for each other reflected in our eyes and neither of us needed words to express them. Indeed, lovers need no language to convey their love to one another!

Nobody Saw Her Struggle

The evening that Jazz found out about my accident, Priyanshi had called her over because she wanted company. The following day, her UPSC results were to be declared and after Randeep, Jazz was her morale booster. By the time Jazz left to talk to Bon, Priyanshi was under a lot of stress—about her results, Jazz and my health. That night, she didn't sleep a wink. Every time she almost fell asleep, she would feel like she was falling and she would abruptly wake up, gasping for air. When the sun was high enough in the sky for the shops to open, she left her apartment and went to a bistro nearby to have breakfast.

The roadside Romeos in her colony knew that she had taken her civil services exams and that she was expecting her results today. Sometimes she wondered how these boys got accurate information about all the girls in their locality.

Not only did they know the goings-on of their lives but also had detailed information about their whereabouts. As Priyanshi walked down the street, she could feel them watching her. She could hear them laughing, scoffing and teasing from the corner of the road. She quickened her pace as she tried to escape their eve-teasing, recalling the incident with Randeep. She had goosebumps on her skin and when she finally reached her apartment, she wasted no time in bolting the door behind her. Was it residual fear from her previous encounter or was it the incessant eve-teasing by these lechers that haunted her, day and night? Could it be fear of failure? Hazy about the meaning of such thoughts, she shut her brain off and tried to isolate herself from the world around her.

She took out her laptop and searched for the results online. Repeatedly, she refreshed the website to check if the results had been declared. Restlessly, she walked in and out of the kitchen and switched between television channels, not settling on any one. Several times, she checked WhatsApp to see if there was any update regarding the results. After all this pressure, would she become the perfect diamond or would she be a decompressed, misshapen stone of no value? She knew that a mob of expectations and responsibilities awaited her, regardless of her result. Once again, she refreshed the website and a sudden rush of blood passed through her body, making her feel light-headed—the results were out. She immediately opened the page and typed in her registration number. The result was just a click away. Before clicking, she prayed to the Almighty for success. With cold hands, she clicked 'GO' and her result was displayed in bold letters.

Priyanshi: FAILED

Her mouth fell open in shock. She sat motionless in front of the screen for a long time. One by one, all the promises she had made to her parents and friends rang in her ears. Failure is the hardest emotional hurdle and Priyanshi now testament to that. Guilt started weighing heavily on her; embarrassment and disgust made her skin crawl. Expressionless, she closed her eyes in grief when her phone rang. It was her dad. She knew what the call was about and instead of responding, she wanted to throw her phone away, far, far away. Her family's doubts about her being a failure were now confirmed; she had let them all down. Her mental stability crumbled under the weight of their high expectations and she was left with no choice but to face reality. Hesitantly, she answered the call. Her father's voice boomed from the other end.

'Beta, did you clear your exams? What's your result?' He opened on a diplomatic note. No 'Hi, hello, how are you? We've missed you.'

Silence!

'What happened?' he asked.

Still silence and the occasional murmur!

'I didn't clear them,' Priyanshi mumbled.

'What did you say?' her dad repeated.

'I failed.'

'Did you just say that you failed?'

Priyanshi replied in a small voice, 'Yes.'

'Do you realize the impact of this on our family's status and reputation? We warned you, Priyanshi, that you should simply come back to Guwahati and that there is no need for such exams, but you were overconfident about yourself. Now having insulted yourself and your family, you will return home. Right?'

'I won't,' Priyanshi said, feebly.

'Oh great, so you mean you need some more time to take the exams again and waste your life and our money. How could you be so foolish? Not to mention selfish? You have already wasted a crucial year of your life, and uncaring of the disappointment that you have caused us, you want to waste another year in the same manner? Look at Randeep, he has already flown to the US and is focused on his career and here you are, still taking exams.

There is no need for another attempt. Come back. I will book your return ticket tonight and you will be home tomorrow.'

'Can I talk to Mom?' Priyanshi pleaded in fear, hoping to change her mother's mind first, and she could then convince her stubborn father.

When Priyanshi's mother came on the line, she had nothing different to say.

'Come back, that's our final decision. Enough of this education and exams. I've asked your uncle to find a job for you here.'

'Mom, you too?' she cried.

She felt like her soul had been crushed. A negative feeling washed over her, a feeling of neglect and dejection. Her dreams of becoming an IAS officer were shattered. Her loneliness knew no bounds when she found that all her dreams had only been a mirage. She couldn't remember if she had a reason to live any more. She browsed Facebook, and came across a status about clearing the exams, uploaded by one of her coaching-class friends. Lost and feeble, she posted a Facebook status too.

An average teenager, a normal human being,
Facing pressure and trauma every day.
Physically, socially and emotionally.

Until the day she faced failure;
And then, no one ever saw her again!

Her parents had rejected her, her hopes had been neglected and her dreams had been slaughtered brutally. Although she had expected her parents to react this way, she had still hoped that they would relent at least this time. After the phone call they were, in a way, dead to her. Jazz was not there to console her, nor was Randeep available to fill her up with positive thoughts again. Each molecule of her body cursed her and she decided to end her life. Frustrated with her life, for more reasons than she could count, she had no will left to survive. The guilt of taking this decision stopped her from calling Randeep but she tried contacting Jazz several times. However, her phone was switched off as she was outside the operation theatre. With no response from Jazz, she forced herself to dial Randeep's number, but he must have been sleeping, as it was night-time in the US. This depressed her further and she wrote a message to Jazz.

I don't know where to start, but all I can think of
currently is that when you read this message, I might

have gone too far. There is a chance that you will be furious as you care for me. Please inform Randeep too. You both have loved me a lot and are the only ones to support me. I had promised Aditya that you would be with him forever and I'm happy that I could at least achieve one thing successfully. It hurts to say this but I failed at the rest. I didn't clear my exam and while I say this, I'm not just referring to the UPSC exam; I'm talking about the test of life itself. I have no complaints, but I feel like I'm not meant for this world. There is an infinite void within me and it's killing me every day, slowly, bit by bit. Which is why I'm ending things here. I am sure Aditya will always keep you happy like he promised me he would, and don't worry, he will be perfectly all right. Apologize to Randeep on my behalf; tell him I'm sorry that I'm leaving without meeting him. No one knows my pain or how often I have cried. I don't want anyone to feel sorry for me. I don't want any attention, but people have always disrespected me for various reasons and that hurts. I have tried my best to hide that hurt, but that hurts too. Say sorry to my mother as I couldn't make her happy and apologize to my dad for not being a daughter he could be proud of. But tell them I loved them like no others. Tell them that I tried repeatedly, but I lost—at everything. Someone has wrongly said that people appreciate your effort and not the result. I don't hate anyone but sitting here, right now, I hate myself. Goodbye forever. I will miss you from above.

Priyanshi sent the message but it remained undelivered. She waited a while before switching her phone off. She took out all the sleeping pills she had and swallowed them in one go. After a few minutes it became difficult for her to breathe and she started suffocating. She was choking and could comprehend the loss of light as she took her last breath. Priyanshi struggled in the last minutes of her life after consuming the pills and the outcome was inevitable. Her body was shutting down, taking away what little energy she had left. Her heart stopped beating eventually and, after a while, her brain cells died. Lifeless, she lay on the floor as darkness surrounded the room, and her life.

When a loved one departs, they leave behind a wound in your life that can never be healed. It was impossible to accept that Priyanshi had left the world behind.

Later that evening, when the security guard rang her doorbell continuously to hand over a letter and no one answered, he grew suspicious and informed the neighbours. They tried calling Priyanshi but her phone was switched off, so they broke the lock open to see if she was okay. They were shocked to find Priyanshi's lifeless body lying on the floor. Immediately, they informed her parents, who went into a state of trauma. Without wasting time, they flew to Delhi. In the meantime, the police was called for a routine inquiry and they found a suicide note and the message. A few hours later, when her parents arrived, they found the sight of their dead daughter unbearable. No matter what they might have said and how they might have acted, she was, at the end of the day, their child—and no parent wants to see their child die. It was a heart-wrenching moment for them, which left a permanent scar on their lives.

After being subjected to regular police inquiry, they took her to the hospital to collect the clearance certificate. Priyanshi's mom had a breakdown but her dad tried his best to be emotionally strong. He blamed himself for his daughter's drastic action. Priyanshi's mom tried calling Jazz and Randeep, but neither of them was available. She did not know where Jazz lived either. By the time they completed all the formalities, it was early morning. As Priyanshi's coffin departed from Delhi, Jazz's flight landed. Jazz had no clue that she would never see Priyanshi again. People believed that she committed suicide as she failed her exams but no one knew the pain she had been going through since she had arrived in Delhi. Along with her, that pain and suffering had come to an end too. Priyanshi was no longer a part of this world which had often mistreated her. Death does not occur when your heart stops beating. It occurs when your heart no longer has a reason to beat.

July 2015
Bandra

The saddest part about people leaving is that they leave memories of themselves behind and, more often than not, we are left longing for more time with the person so that we can create more memories. What is terrifying, though, is when you try to remember someone and recollect all the memories you have of them, you see everything except their face. Every single one of us was upset, including Roma, who hadn't even met Priyanshi. There was silence at the table, not because the restaurant was about to close and people were leaving, but because the scars from our past hadn't completely healed yet, compelling us into a silence from which it was hard to break out. Some wounds never heal completely, and on days like this, they bleed and hurt again.

'I simply cannot believe Priyanshi is no more. For the last few hours, I have lived her life. In fact, I was going to ask you if she was coming to the wedding and whether you could introduce me to the girl who made it all possible,' Roma said mournfully.

'She will stay in our hearts forever. Although I spent less time with her than Jazz did, I always felt that she had become my friend first. The way she supported me, even when I was at fault, was nothing short of incredible. Every second of our relationship became possible only because of her.' On hearing my reply to Roma, Jazz excused herself for some time; she always got overwhelmed when we spoke of Priyanshi, and we all understood, because we went through the same thing as well.

'How did Jazz come to know about Priyanshi?' Roma inquired.

Taking a deep breath, I continued telling my story. 'When Jazz returned to Delhi, she was completely exhausted. When she finally switched on her cell phone, all her pending messages and WhatsApp chats were delivered in one go. That's when she read Priyanshi's final message. She rushed to Priyanshi's apartment but saw that it was locked. Finding that strange, she called Priyanshi; her phone was switched off. When she inquired with the neighbours, they told her of Priyanshi's death. Jazz couldn't believe it. Heartbroken, she tried to contact Priyanshi's parents but it was too late, as the last rites had already taken place. I still feel terrible because when both of them needed me the most, I wasn't there. Bon consoled Jazz and looked after her mentally, physically and emotionally.'

Jazz loved Priyanshi more than she ever knew. Priyanshi was a friend she could trust and who always listened; she was the one who brought love to her life, the one who was more than just a friend; their friendship, in a lot of ways, ran thicker than blood. No words could completely explain what Priyanshi had meant to Jazz. She didn't even get a chance to say goodbye. Priyanshi was living a lie, hiding her true emotions behind a mask, and none of us ever saw through it. Little did we know about the latent pain and hurt that she had been living with. Jazz fervently wished that she could go back in time and do something about it, or at least see her and hug her one last time. If Bon hadn't been a pillar of strength for her, Jazz would've had an emotional breakdown. As Jazz returned to the table, I looked tenderly at her and, wiping away her tears, I held her hand.

It was nearly closing time. I saw that a handful people at the other tables were still finishing their drinks. Roma excused herself to go to the washroom while I poured a final round for everyone.

'Check, please?' I signalled the waiter. 'But once we are done with the drinks.'

'No problem, sir.' He refilled our glasses with water and left.

As we were finishing the last bits of the biryani, Roma returned.

'Did you tell him then?' Roma asked Jazz. 'About Priyanshi?'

'Yes, I had to. But I disclosed it to him a few days after he was discharged from the hospital. I didn't want him to be stressed, or the doctors would have delayed the discharge date and I desperately wanted him to be able to go home. I cannot explain what it was like when he was hospitalized.' Jazz paused for a moment to take a deep breath. Even though it had happened a long time ago, the painful memories were still sharp in her mind. 'When I told him about Priyanshi, he was extremely angry that I hadn't told him sooner.'

I continued, 'I felt so helpless. I just couldn't digest the news that Priyanshi had left us forever. I wanted to fly to Delhi the minute I heard, but my situation was such that I couldn't even walk because of the plate inserted in my leg. It's still there.' I pointed to my left leg and added, 'The doctors had advised bed rest for several months. Complete bed rest. Still, I tried to bring a smile to her face whenever I could.'

Roma glanced at my leg and said, 'It must have been difficult, I'm sure. How did you cope? I would have given up.'

'I had no choice. The worst part was the trauma that followed. I used to wake up in the middle of the night in shock and it scared me. After regaining consciousness in the hospital, I realized that I couldn't even walk without help. I was dependent on someone all the time, even to use the washroom. That depressed me. The circumstances were discouraging and all I wanted was to run away from the hospital, except I couldn't. Every now and then my leg would spasm in pain so badly that I would have to stay in the same position for hours. The initial days were scary, until the doctors and physiotherapists taught me how to walk on one leg with a walker. Once they saw I was confident enough, they discharged me. But I wasn't allowed to use the walker for the first few weeks after being discharged.'

'But, by God's grace, you can run a marathon now,' Jazz added.

'I would rather not take that risk.' I laughed.

'Anyway, I'm glad you both never fought again after that. You were meant to be together always. So I hope you never think of breaking up.' Roma heaved a sigh of relief.

Jazz and I quickly glanced at each other and burst out laughing.

No fights? Seriously? That's really possible? Not with us at least.

Roma sensed something fishy and said, 'Don't tell me you did. *Really?*'

We laughed louder this time and I continued, 'Yes. We broke up . . . almost . . . again.'

'Forever' Is a Myth?

You know it is true love when you cannot imagine a future for yourself without your significant other in it. It's when you feel content with just one smile from her. It's when you can't sleep when she is beside you and, even after getting lost in her eyes for hours, you don't feel tired. My relationship with Jazz had all these traits until my accident and Priyanshi's death. Bon and I did everything we could to help Jazz get back to normal again. We did our best to make her see that she could turn Priyanshi's loss into a strength, by living her life the way Priyanshi would have wanted her to—by being happy and jovial, just like Jazz had always been.

With our constant support and encouragement, Jazz transformed all her negative feelings and channelled them into her work, with a new-found passion and ambition to achieve more. Not only did she get a new job with a huge salary hike, she also secured a very respectable position at Aon Hewitt in Gurgaon. Within a month of starting work there, she was given the best employee award from amongst hundreds of other employees, which paved the way for further success when she was promoted for critical meetings and tasks, where once again she handled everything with ease. In the meantime, while I was happy and supportive of her success, I also became insecure about my future. About a month after my operation, my dependency on others hadn't decreased. My physiotherapy had already begun by then, but I still wasn't comfortable. For even the smallest thing, I had to wait until someone heard me call out. Each day I felt more challenged, and my hopes of recovery began to diminish. One time, my physiotherapist made me use the walker till the washroom, but his constant scrutiny made me feel like a loser. Negative thoughts started clouding my judgment, round the clock, and I started to believe that I was no longer worthy of Jazz. I started to believe that our relationship was a mismatch and she deserved someone better.

'How is my patient feeling today? Did he take his medicines?' Jazz cooed at me during one of our Skype calls.

'Not that great,' I grumbled.

'Not that bad either, right?' She was trying so hard to be encouraging that I almost felt guilty for not feeling better.

'You can say that. Anyway, are you leaving for work?' I asked, trying to change the subject.

'I'm waiting for the cab. I'm ready and you can appreciate my new dress if you want,' she said, backing away from the camera so I could see a full-length image of her.

'You look ravishing as always, Jazz. Now I won't look good next to you holding a stick.' I sighed.

'Shut up. Why do you have to say that? In a few weeks, you will be walking just like you used to before. If something like that had happened to me, would you have left me?' Jazz admonished.

'I wouldn't . . . but . . . you know how it feels.'

'I won't listen to any of it. Stop talking nonsense. Nothing has changed between us. I still love you like before.' She said it all in one breath.

I remained silent.

'Nothing has changed . . . right?' Jazz repeated, hesitatingly.

'No,' I lied.

'Good. I have to go now, my cab's here. Bye!' She gave me a flying kiss and disconnected the call. Though she loved me selflessly, more than I could have ever imagined, my insecurities flared up, making me forget everything and act irrationally. I hid these insecurities from Jazz because I didn't want to upset her. Jazz must have sensed this, which is why she asked me to write down my fears and then tear the paper apart. Instead of ripping up what I had written, I carefully kept the paper under my pillow, allowing it to hurt me. Sleepless nights, the physical as well as mental pain—I was bearing it all, unsure of how much longer I could go on this way.

She loves me. But she deserves better. I am a burden. The doctor says I will recover in a few months, and if I take my physiotherapy seriously, I'll recover even quicker. I did take his advice seriously but it gets harder with each day. Jazz is growing and succeeding in every aspect, her life is in fast-forward, whereas I'm learning how to walk again at a snail's pace. I think it's better we part ways before I hurt her.

My days were filled with thoughts like these. Every time I tried to divert my mind from them, these thoughts would come rushing back at full speed. These lingering thoughts, as well as the post-traumatic stress, had now become a part of my daily life. Every time I managed to sleep for a few hours, the shock of the accident would take over and I'd wake up frightened. The accident and the pain kept coming back to me as I relived it, over and over again, every time I went to sleep. This would keep me awake through the night, and the lack of sleep would attract weird thoughts which had started to infect my love. It was a vicious cycle and, day by day, it was getting harder for me to pull myself out of it.

Someone help. Pull me out! an inner voice inside me screamed. These screams went unheard by the world. Nothing seemed real except for a few positive words from Jazz.

'I have a holiday coming up. A long weekend,' she said one day, after coming back from work.

'Wow, you should go somewhere, maybe,' I dully suggested.

'Yes, you got me. I'm planning a trip to Mumbai,' she said excitedly.

'What's the use? I can't even drive or go anywhere far.' It had become harder for me to keep the dejection from creeping into my tone.

'I will take you,' she said, chirpily.

'I don't know . . .' I sighed.

'You've started again? Anyway, I have news. There was a competition held on my floor and the winners were to be given priority training. Guess what? I won!' Jazz said.

'No wonder.'

'The reward is if I do well in training, I will be applicable for IJPs this year. Isn't that great?'

'Yeah.'

After the initial positive conversation at the beginning, the latter part added to my frustration. I was not jealous of her success. In fact, I was happier than she was and was extremely proud of her, but each step that she took ahead only added to our differences. I felt a growing gap between us. She forwarded me the email she had received after winning the competition.

> *Subject: Mid-Week Competition for Priority Training*
> *Hi Team,*
> *Thank you for participating in the mid-week competition today. It was an hour well spent with everyone. Congratulations to Jazz on winning the competition. Great job! We will keep you posted regarding the details of the training.*
> *Thanks,*
> *Client Services Manager*
> *Aon Hewitt*

I should have been happy but I was shit-scared. Her thoughts and hard work were reflecting in her success, whereas my thoughts added no value to my life. I never imagined that after writing so many books, my mind would stop working. I was scared because my thought process—which happened to be my only avenue to surviving as a writer—had shut. The email added fuel to the burning emotions inside me and I could no longer keep them hidden. I wrote to her soon after.

> *Jazz, you're still my everything and I'm still yours. I have never ever met a person like you before and*

I have no hesitation in saying so. You are the most loyal girlfriend anyone could ask for. Long-distance relationships are difficult but we surpassed all the big obstacles they have to offer but overlooked a small stone on the way. I want to confess to you that I don't deserve you or your love. You are excelling so wonderfully and you deserve someone who can do the same. I know I have hurt you because of my thoughts, but I wish you knew that every night I fall asleep crying because I am not good enough for you. I am afraid and I'm tired of waiting for the day when you realize that you deserve someone better, which is why I am telling you this now.

Within minutes she replied.

Either stop your bullshit or kill me forever. I'm coming to Mumbai whether you like it or not. Stop hurting me and yourself like this. I've had it.

My depressing attitude had hurt her before too but I didn't want to break her heart. I requested her not to come to Mumbai as this feeling had me caged. But she believed in me more than I believed in myself, and even though I continued to share these negative feelings with her, not once did her confidence in me waver. Was I thinking these thoughts because nothing good had happened to me in the recent past and I didn't know how to handle it? I thought our story would be a long series, but it seemed like it was nearing its end. When it was time for Jazz to come to Mumbai, I became very sceptical of a happily ever after. What happens to 'forever'? Is it one great big lie then? I wasn't sure if my love story was going to come to an abrupt anti-climax. I was only sure of this—either this was the start of a new beginning or the beginning of the end.

Not Just a Relationship, It's a *Realationship*

We can fight against the entire world but to win a battle against ourselves is a nearly impossible task, especially in a world of our own creation, where all our memories and insecurities reside. I tried expressing this to Jazz when she came to Mumbai a couple of days later. During that period, my physiotherapist made me walk around the house with a walker, although, mentally, I felt paralysed. My body had started the healing process, but I was still plagued by nightmares from the accident. I also experienced mental unrest due to the increasing differences between me and Jazz. I had nothing to do and had to sit in one place all day. After a traumatic experience, your physical injuries begin to heal; it's your mind that starts malfunctioning and takes longer to recover from the trauma.

Despite my parents' best attempts, I remained stubbornly depressed, though it wasn't intentional and despite the fact that I was physically getting better. Maybe, the dependency on others had shaken my belief in myself to the very core.

However, the day Jazz was supposed to meet me, I felt genuine excitement. My fear and insecurities took a backseat. The moment she rang the bell, I wanted to rush to open the door, but I couldn't. My mom opened the door and I could hear them whispering. I could hear a third voice whispering too. On listening closely, I realized it was Dipika. My mother proceeded to inquire after Dipika's welfare. With each second I grew more impatient to see Jazz. But Mom wouldn't stop quizzing them about this and that. When I couldn't wait any more, I slowly started to get up from my bed. With the help of the walker and with the pace of a tortoise, I walked to the living room. Only I knew how desperately I wanted to see her, catch a glimpse of her smile, look into her eyes, revel in her innocence and basically spend some time with her in person! As I walked through the door, I caught a glimpse of bliss. She looked like poetry with her elegant smile, her eyes rhyming. Unaware of my presence, she kept smiling while my mom talked to Dipika, occasionally asking Jazz a question to include her in the conversation.

As my walker scraped across the floor, Jazz saw me. She stood up but restrained herself from rushing over to hug me in my mom's presence. Once I was seated comfortably on the sofa with some help, Mom excused herself and went inside.

'I have decided. When I get married to you and move to Mumbai, we will explore a new place every weekend. We'll go to different lounges, on long drives, try a variety of foods and get a taste of the local cuisine too,' Jazz declared.

I was shocked. Did she say 'marry'? Was she proposing to me? 'Are you sure?' I asked her.

'Yes. I love vada pav.' Her excitement reflected in her words. Then lowering her voice, she added, 'And you.'

She got up, walked over and sat beside me. Holding my hand, after ensuring that my mom wasn't watching, she smiled at me. Dipika acted as a human shield, blocking the view from Mom's room. I couldn't stop smiling at the way she stood.

'Do you have an objection?' Dipika asked.

'No,' I replied, grinning from ear to ear.

'Then concentrate on holding her hand. You can take it one step ahead too. I don't mind,' Dipika teased.

'You seem more desperate than us. I think *you* should get married soon,' I joked.

'Find me a rich boyfriend so we can go to Hawaii for the honeymoon.' She laughed.

'That shall be our first task as a married couple, Dipika. We'll set you up with the most eligible bachelors from our friend circle and you can have your pick!' Jazz told her.

Our friendly banter went on for some time and I realized that, for the first time since my accident, I was genuinely happy. All these days I had been rather morose and depressed. Jazz sensed it too and said, 'Aditya, lately you have been giving in to negativity. You've been letting your thoughts win. But you don't have to; your thoughts only have the strength to overpower you if you let them. I know the last few weeks have been hard for you. It's one of those times when luck is not on your side. But remember that I'll always be by your side. And you know how capable you are, look at your achievements and take strength from that knowledge and move on with confidence.'

Jazz pointed towards the awards displayed in my living room. I stared at them for a while and sighed. 'I really don't know what lies ahead for me.'

'Trust Waheguruji, trust the universe, trust life and, above all, trust yourself.'

'I trust you. I love you.'

'I love you too.'

She hugged me, while Dipika still maintained her ridiculous position as a human shield.

'Are you guys done? My legs are starting to hurt,' she exclaimed. We laughed and I felt my old, happy self returning.

Even if it was only for a few minutes, Jazz's presence gave me a reason to continue living. To love again. Romance is when you sit beside her and don't say anything, but her presence is enough to comfort your thoughts. It's when your hearts meet in silence, tied by mutual trust. For us, more than roses, passionate kisses and intimacy, the silences we shared were most cherished. Over time, we found that nothing was more romantic than sitting next to each other, simply enjoying each other's company. Jazz made me walk around the living room, first with the walker and then for some time without it as she held me on one side and became my support.

'I won't be able to.' I panicked when she replaced my walker with herself.

'Do you trust me?' she asked, and I nodded. She continued, 'Then, just walk.'

I don't know how she supported me, even though I had lost a lot of weight over the past few months. That probably helped. But her confidence in me made me double my efforts, as I didn't want to disappoint her. She helped me balance as I walked on one leg for another five rounds of the living room. Conscious of the pain I might be causing her by resting my weight on her, I quickened my pace, which was exactly what she wanted.

'I can endure all the pain if that helps bring back a sense of normalcy to your life . That wasn't so hard, was it?' she asked, expectantly.

'I am sorry. Did I hurt you?' I felt guilty.

'Shut up.'

All this while, Dipika and my mom had been observing us and the happiness in my mom's eyes was incomparable. After a long time, she was watching me walk without a walker. She allowed Dipika and Jazz to take me outside for a walk but with a walker this time and asked us to be careful. The day, so far, had been perfect. For me, it was memorable, something that was imprinted in my mind forever.

Carefully, Jazz helped me into a cab and took me to D'Crepes Café in Hiranandani Meadows. It took us a while to get there and Dipika had already reached by the time we arrived, as Jazz had instructed her to go ahead. There was something fishy about the way they glanced at each other sneakily and had a secretive conversation. Despite me asking about it several times, Jazz didn't reveal a thing. But the moment we reached the cafe, I was taken by surprise. I was on cloud nine. I couldn't believe what I was seeing.

The café was beautifully decorated with white and red balloons, red roses and a big banner on the wall with the message, 'Get well soon, my love'. Jazz had booked the entire café for an hour, made possible by Dipika's friendship with the owner. There were floating candles and fairy lights that added to the romantic ambience of the café.

'You think you're the only one who can plan such things?' Jazz grinned. She took me by the hand and led the way. 'Come on.'

'This is all for me?' I asked, feeling special and cherished.

'Yes, I decided to try my hand at this because you do so much for me.' Jazz pulled my cheeks as we sat down. Dipika had helped Jazz with all the arrangements and it was flawless. Within moments, the manager welcomed me with a plate of their special pastries and a card.

I glanced at Jazz who was beaming at me with eyes that radiated the purest form of love. I opened the envelope and saw a collage of all our pictures with a message at the bottom.

I want you to know that I believe in you. I just want you to know that I'll be there beside you through both the good times and the bad. I'll be your light when the road gets dark. I'll lend a shoulder when you feel weak. I know you can do it all alone, but I'll never hesitate to encourage you and be by your side. I also want you to know that you complete me and make my life amazing. This world is a better place just because of you, as you make me feel beautiful. I am thankful to you for what I have and everything that we will have together. You are the only man I ever want to share my life with. I could never imagine what it would be like if we were to lose each other. I don't even want to think about it. All I want to think of is you and our time together. I will love you till I breathe my last and, hopefully, when that day comes, you will still find me in your arms. When we turn old, we will look back and laugh at the times when we argued about silly things. Because our love is strong enough to overcome any and all arguments. My love for you will never fade away, remember that, always.

Sitting on the couch, I hugged Jazz passionately, forgetting all about the staff around us. I squeezed her and wished for the moment to last forever. The manager interrupted us by clearing his throat and placing a cake on the table. How could I not love this girl who knew what it means to be loved? She was giving me new relationship goals by making my life worth living. She completed me that day and extinguished all the negativity that had haunted me. There was no space for it any more, my soul was hers!

'I wish Priyanshi was here,' she said quietly.

'She is looking at both of you right now and I'm sure she's proud of her girl,' Dipika said, sitting across from Jazz and me.

'She was the one who was in support of us being together from the very start. She was the reason I gave you a second chance. I never knew that it would turn out to be the best gamble of my life!' Jazz said with damp eyes.

'I never told you but every time we fought, she was the one who consoled me and told me of ways to pamper you. She also gave me live updates of your reactions when sitting beside you; she was a sweetheart, a gem of a person,' I said, visualizing her with us at that moment.

That was the best evening I'd had in several months. Your world suddenly shines bright when you are with your loved ones. Jazz was a powerhouse of energy, love and compassion. The happiness radiant on my mom and dad's faces when we returned home delighted me. They hugged me and showered kisses on me, like excited parents when they see their child walking on his own for the very first time. He may fall, get up and fall again, but the pride at him walking alone is what makes it all worth it. Jazz had already won over my parents, without me even having to try! There was indeed more to her than the eyes could see. She was like a book that you can't stop reading. This time around, I was confident; I knew that Jazz and my story would end in a happily ever after!

July 2015
Bandra

'I think we should make a move now,' Jazz said, looking at the time. The restaurant we were in was now almost empty.

'It was one hell of an evening,' Roma exclaimed.

I grinned and paid the manager, tipping heavily as he had allowed us to sit without any disturbance. As I rose from the chair, I winced in pain and looked at my operated leg. I moved my ankle in circles and, almost immediately, the pain disappeared. Maybe I was imagining the pain, especially after telling Roma about the accident.

I never looked back after the day Jazz visited me. She stood by me through thick and thin and relentlessly inspired me, encouraged me and loved me. Within a few months, I was running on a treadmill without any fear of falling down. Indeed, love makes you better and more confident if you are with right person. Everyone, including my parents, played a massive role in helping me build my second life and Jazz was at the centre of it all.

As we went downstairs, Roma bombarded me with another question, 'So, do you think your parents would agree after today?'

'I wish I could answer confidently, but the truth is I don't know yet. Even my four years of engineering becomes useless when I think of a possible answer to this question.' I laughed.

'I think they've agreed. Or else you wouldn't have met Jazz today,' Roma said.

'How?' Dipika asked.

'Let's not get into it,' Jazz replied, not wanting to burst the bubble.

'Yes, they have. Else they would have objected outwardly. Moreover, it was not as if Jazz had come in out of the blue. They had met her a couple of times before, it's just that they assumed her to be a friend. I'm glad the inter-caste melodrama didn't come into the picture.'

'That's meant for Bollywood.' Roma winked.

'True!' Dipika laughed.

'But your story is no less than a Bollywood movie!' Roma pointed towards me and laughed. We all did.

'You can't say that. More than our parents objecting, we never thought we would come this far in a long-distance relationship. We had only heard of the problems faced in one.'

'But people like you do exist,' Jazz said, hugging me.

'Indeed,' I proudly declared.

'What about your parents?' Roma questioned Jazz once we sat in the car.

'I actually told them about wanting to get married before I told this idiot and that scared me. Bon told them everything before going back to the US and, touch wood, they agreed without even meeting Aditya. They love me a lot and they trust me to not take a step that would hurt them. My dad is my hero and my mom's the best too. Dad recently had a word with Aditya and asked him to check with his parents if they were okay with an inter–caste marriage. It's because of them that I've been after Aditya's life to reveal our relationship to his parents. Now everything has been sorted out.'

'They didn't ask to meet Aditya even once?' Roma asked, incredulous.

'He was interrogated for two straight hours on Skype. It was nothing less than a CBI interrogation. After that, his profile was verified to check if he was genuine and past records were analysed to rate his loyalty. The biggest issue was, of course, his profession, as my parents were a little confused about what he does, being a writer.'

'Probably watches *Sooryavansham* on Sony or *Savdhaan India* on Life OK?' Dipika laughed.

'Fuck off! I don't watch that crap!' I exclaimed.

'Dipika, you should write our love story. You've always wanted to write,' Jazz suggested.

'Thanks, but no thanks. I'm better at what I'm currently doing. Recruiting people as a HR manager is my calling, not writing. Let Aditya write it. He can write your love scenes pretty well. He'll have first-hand experience too!' Dipika winked, making Jazz blush.

'I'm going to throw you out of this car now!' I joked, looking at her in the mirror.

'Fuck off.'

We soon reached Dipika's apartment and the girls got out of the car. When I glanced at Jazz, I realized how fortunate I was to have her in my life. We had a relationship where we never kept secrets or had to pretend. It was a pure relationship where, even though we fought and argued, we also kissed and hugged; we Skyped, WhatsApped and tagged each other on Facebook; we talked, laughed and cried, but, through it all, what kept us going was that we loved each other! That's just how it was with us. From putting each other on hold during phone calls, we were about to hold each other for a lifetime. From blocking each other on WhatsApp, we were about to get rid of the obstructions between us!

When you say the words 'long distance', the next thing that comes to mind is 'relationship'. You imagine falling asleep on Skype or chatting late at night on WhatsApp. It's said you can't really know someone until you meet them in person. But Jazz and I have met in more ways than I can count. Not in the stereotypical, conventional way, but from a distance. She has seen me snore when I've been tired. I have seen her eyes glitter when she talks about her job and the things she loves. Tired, when I reach home, her voice is already on my laptop speakers. On my laptop screen, I have met the teddy bear in her room. We have met more through than in real life, so we cannot believe that technology ruins lives. It's been saving ours all this while!

217

Roma's voice brought me back to reality. 'Bye guys. I really had a memorable time with all of you. I wish you both a great life ahead.'

'You must come to our engagement party! I'll send your formal invite through Dipika,' Jazz announced.

'I would have come anyway. But is Randeep also coming? I want to meet him too.'

'Yes. He will be there.'

She grinned and walked towards her apartment but, realizing she'd missed asking her final question of the day, she turned back and shouted, 'Aditya, when are you getting engaged?'

'Enough questions for today. Goodnight, Roma.' I winked and drove off.

End of Bachelor Life; Hello, Wife

27 November 2015
Delhi

Those who were unaware of our relationship asked us whether it was a love marriage or an arranged marriage. I wanted to ask them their definitions of both because I never believed in differentiating between the two. Be it love or arranged, marriage is love; a warm and beautiful commitment to each other and with God. It's an endurance, which is a new discovery every day; it's a harmony of two hearts, acceptance of two minds and solidarity of two souls.

My entire family, along with our friends, were in Delhi to witness me getting into the smallest pair of handcuffs. Jazz and I were getting engaged the following day and our families were having a small get-together the night before.

Of course, we were in each other's presence, but our long-distance affair continued as she sat at one end of the table and I at the other, exchanging discreet glances occasionally. Thankfully, we had our own personal saviours in our hands—our mobile phones!

'Holy shit, we are getting exchanged . . . oh sorry, engaged! ☺' I texted her.

Her reply came within seconds. 'Guess what? I just lost my boyfriend! He is my fiancé now.'

Our smiles were indicative of how happy we were. Every fight, every tantrum had been worth it because it had resulted in this day. We had to limit our texts—Jazz's mom, my soon-to-be mother-in-law, kept glancing at my phone and I didn't want to land myself in an embarrassing situation with her. According to tradition, she had to sit with my family and I with hers.

'Beta, I wanted to tell you one thing,' Jazz's mom said, looking at me.

For a moment, I was petrified that she had read one of the texts.

'You know, Jazz is a completely spoilt girl . . . pampered . . . Dad's princess.'

No one knows better than me, Mom, how spoilt she is. I can even make a list!

'You need to take a little extra care of her, the way she dresses, her shopping and . . . '

220

Oh, don't get me started on her five-minute theory.

'As a girl's mother, I'm just a little bit anxious.'

I should be the one who's afraid. Your worries are practically over; mine begin now!

'Don't worry, Mom. I know this and I'll make sure she stays content in Mumbai. I will be there and you can trust me. Also, I have no problem with what she wears and neither will my parents. I will not stop her from doing what she wants,' I assured her.

'Thank you, beta.' She embraced me.

It is not that difficult to convince a mother-in-law. I felt proud of myself. But I now had added responsibilities; it wasn't just going to be me any more. We discussed various things about the wedding, from fixing a date to the clothes. I had to admit Punjabis liked planning things way ahead of time, but they were warm and lovable.

The food was served shortly. There was an array of tandoori chicken, fish fry, prawns, chicken tikka, mutton and, of course, alcohol.

One of the advantages of marrying a Punjabi. You can get delicious chicken for a lifetime and a mini bar with a permit licence.

As I worked on the chicken and prawns, I received a call from a friend with whom I spoke in Marathi.

An obvious concern from her mom followed. 'All of you speak in Marathi. Jazz won't understand a word. She'll be alone the entire day. For her sake please speak in Hindi too. Otherwise she will feel completely isolated.'

'Mom, leave it to me. Keeping her happy, making her smile and fulfilling all her wishes is not only my duty but my privilege.'

As a mother, her concerns were valid. It's not easy for a girl's family to just hand over their precious daughter to someone with blind trust assuming he would protect and cherish her the same way as they have for more than two decades. It's perhaps the saddest and happiest day for a mother to let her daughter go. It may seem like just yesterday she was watching her take her first step and now she's watching her walk down the aisle to her future husband. For a father, it's even worse. Jazz's dad looked so concerned and was on his toes the entire time, making sure all the arrangements were up to the mark. On the inside, he must have been mourning the fact that his daughter will no longer make him tea every morning.

I saw her dad walking towards me and I stood up. 'As the engagement is taking place in the Punjabi tradition, you have to wear a turban. Will you be comfortable with that?' He saw me staring blankly and added, 'You can remove it after the prayers. That's okay.'

'No . . . no. I was just thinking of something else.' I paused. I thought to myself, *I already have a beard and now a turban—a complete Punjabi.* 'It's an honour, Dad, and I won't remove it. It's just that somebody will have to help me tie one as I don't know how to.'

'That's not a problem. I'll do it for you.'

'Thank you.'

The content and pleased look after I agreed didn't leave his face all evening, which brought about a classic end to the night.

'Have you gone nuts? Fuck dude, if anyone comes to know, it'll be the end of my engagement. This is crazy,' I shouted.

'No one will know. Everyone is almost asleep. And I'll drop them off,' Randeep coaxed me.

'Is Dipika also coming?' I asked, apprehensive of his plan.

'Yeah, and her sister too.'

'You can't be serious, man.'

Randeep and I were sharing a room at the hotel where my entire family was staying for the engagement and he was up to another fucking adventure. Jazz wanted to drink and insisted that Randeep arrange it. He, in turn, called them to the hotel, thus putting my engagement at stake.

Such a rascal, I thought as he went to pick them up. Unfortunately, Jazz and the group had agreed to this stunt.

After everyone had gone to sleep at her home, they sneaked out through the back exit and successfully escaped without anyone noticing. Our hotel was not far from her house and by the time they were outside the gate, Randeep was waiting for them in his car. The three girls got inside and Randeep sped back to the hotel.

'You are exactly as I imagined,' Roma commented.

'Pardon?' Randeep looked confused.

'Aditya, Jazz and I narrated their love story to her a few months ago and she's been wanting to meet you ever since.' Dipika laughed.

Before Randeep could react, they'd reached the hotel. Once assured that no one who knew them was around, they parked the car and tiptoed through the lobby, reaching our room. All the while I'd been waiting restlessly, and the moment I heard the doorbell, I rushed to let them in.

'Thank God you are here.'

'I thought you weren't excited about this idea,' Randeep taunted.

'You are a real pain in my ass. Such a . . .'

He opened the beer cans and handed them out before I could say anything further.

After an hour or so, we were all drunk.

This is a final cheers to my bachelorhood.

'I don't know why, but it feels like something is missing,' Randeep said, suddenly.

'Priyanshi,' Jazz whispered, saying what everyone had been thinking.

'How did you feel when you found out?' Roma asked Randeep.

'I felt guilty. Guilty for not answering her last call as I was fast asleep. Guilty for not being in India and for not being able to meet her. Guilty for not being with Jazz when Aditya was hospitalized . . . If I had answered that call, everything would be different. She would have been here with us. But that's the saddest part. You cannot control life the way you want to,' Randeep confessed and then proceeded to finish his beer.

'I'm sure she's smiling from above looking at Aditya and Jazz,' Dipika said.

'Oh yes, but we miss you, Priyanshi . . . a lot,' Jazz screamed.

I'm not sure whether Priyanshi heard the cry or not, but someone from the hotel surely did because the next minute there was a knock on the door. I got up to check and while the others held their breath. As I looked through the peephole, my heart jumped out of my mouth. I wanted to take refuge under the blankets or jump from my window to escape. My body froze and, even though everyone was looking at me anxiously, I couldn't utter a word. Not even half a word.

Fuck, fuck! It's over. I can see the end. Randeep, I am going to murder you.

'Who's outside?' Jazz whispered.

'Dad.'

'Yours or hers?' Randeep asked.

Hell, does it matter? The outcome would be same.

'Mine,' I uttered.

'Run . . . run into the bathroom,' Randeep instructed us as Dad rang the bell.

In a flash, I ran into the bathroom with the three girls and locked the door. Randeep hid the cans under the bed and in the drawers. Trying to look as normal as possible, he opened the door wide open.

'I just heard a girl's voice. Did it come from here?' Dad asked.

'A girl? Here? Impossible.'

My father walked inside to see if everything was fine. Though he didn't see any cans, he didn't see me in the room either. He inquired about my absence and Randeep said, 'He has gone for a walk as he was feeling constipated.'

Constipated? Couldn't he find some other excuse? I could hear them through the door and wanted to kill Randeep with the first thing I could lay my hands on.

'No problem. I will call him,' said Dad.

Randeep saw my phone lying on the bed and added, 'He has forgotten his phone here.'

Dad thought for a while and continued to wait. The girls were drunk; I was not in my senses and we had locked ourselves in the bathroom. Randeep was pretending to be the most innocent chap in Delhi and my dad was in no mood to leave.

'Do you believe we're getting engaged tomorrow?' I whispered to Jazz.

'Tomorrow? The twenty-eighth is already here. It's almost quarter to two.' Jazz blushed as if we were on a date and not locked in a bloody bathroom.

'I'm sitting on the commode, not in a garden so don't go getting any ideas.' I panicked.

After we'd spent a unforgettable hour in the bathroom, my dad finally decided to leave.

'He's probably using a public toilet somewhere. Food is generally digested right after a walk,' Randeep commented before my dad left without reacting.

The moment Randeep locked the door, I exited the bathroom and pounced on him, pinning him down on the bed. He struggled to escape my punches and laughed loudly. Randeep decided to drop the girls home before anyone noticed they were gone. I could only breathe peacefully once Jazz messaged that they had reached without any further hitches, but the excitement to getting hitched in a few hours kept me awake the whole night!

She Completed My Love Story

28 November 2015
India Habitat Centre, Delhi

It was almost six in the evening and Delhi was ready to embrace Mumbai. If Punjabis are known for their extravagant lifestyle and big Indian weddings, Maharashtrians aren't too far behind; elegantly classy, they are equally lavish, joyous and bubbly. It was not only a union of two souls but of two families from different religions and cultures. How does that matter when love exists? I had longed to see Jazz all dressed up on this day and to spend eternity with her. I had longed for a time when I could hear only her voice, and now that day wasn't too far away.

'You look very handsome in a sherwani,' Bon commented, looking me over once, while Jazz's dad helped me wear a turban.

My happiness couldn't be expressed in words. My beard aligned with my jaw and the pink turban on my head complimented the black sherwani I was wearing, making me feel like a nawab when I looked in the mirror.

'Do I?' I asked looking at her dad and brother.

'Yes. Wonderful. You look classy, son. Come, let's go inside,' her dad stated.

We were in the changing room and once they adjusted the turban properly, we moved towards the engagement hall through the lobby. I tried to peep into the bride's changing room but couldn't see anything as there were too many girls gathered outside Jazz's room. Anxious to not only see Jazz but to also show my off turban, I went towards where my family, along with hers, seemed to be having a great time.

'Oh my God, you look so different. We couldn't recognize you for a minute!' my mom exclaimed on seeing me, and my dad had a similar reaction.

'I thought Jazz's cousin had arrived,' Randeep teased.

'Navjot Singh Siddhu,' Dipika commented.

'No, Bhai, you look great,' Roma concluded.

Everybody had something to say, but the pleased looks on the faces of Jazz's family and relatives were satisfying. The day belonged to them and Jazz and nothing could be worth more than those happy smiles. Jazz's brother led me on to the stage and made me sit on the regal sofa. Suddenly, all the eyes in the room were on me. It was not only embarrassing but also scary, and made me a little uneasy. My eyes were glued to the entrance as I desperately waited to catch a glimpse of Jazz. There was a blur of striking colour all around as the girls danced, clothed in all the colours of the rainbow; their bright smiles lit up their faces; their feet were decorated with mehendi and, as they spun on their toes, each little movement made me more impatient and excited to see the girl of my dreams. Our love had blossomed, day after day, surviving through the struggles. Our time together had flown by, it seemed, as today we were starting our lives as one.

'Dipika,' Jazz said, turning towards her. 'How do I look?'

'This is the twenty-fifth time she has asked this,' Bon said as he sat on a chair in the dressing room, looking bored.

'Shut up, Bhai.' Jazz glared at him.

'Jazz, you look like a princess! I've never seen anyone look more beautiful!' Dipika exclaimed, adjusting her bangles.

Jazz's father entered and asked everyone to leave for a few minutes as he wanted to talk to Jazz alone.

'Is everything okay?' she asked.

Her dad nodded and waited for everyone to go. This scared Jazz a little bit. Her dad sat beside her and held her hand.

'It is hard to believe that your big day is here. I have waited for this moment since the day you were born, yet I feel unprepared for it. I can never forget the drive to the hospital the day your mom gave birth to you and the drive back home with you in my arms. Remembering all the years we have shared together brings tears to my eyes. I feel like it was only yesterday that I dropped you off to school for the first time. You are a beautiful and loving daughter and I'm proud of the woman you have become.'

'Dad, why are you saying all this? I am and will always remain your daughter first. I am not going away from you,' Jazz said with moist eyes.

'Why am I saying all this? I don't think you will understand. I don't think that your mom could have understood when she got engaged. You probably won't be able to experience these emotions until you have a child of your own. I know you love him dearly, as does he. But never forget that there is a man in this world who loves you more than your fiancé or your husband and that's your father.'

They hugged each other and, a few minutes later, her dad led her out of the dressing room. Finally, Jazz was prepared to enter the hall with grace. Though there were still a few months to the actual wedding, it was a day that held great significance for both of us.

Jazz's mom was pampering her; how could she stay apart from her mother who understood everything without asking to be understood in return? Her brother hugged her; she'd had numerous fights with him as a kid but now these were memories that would be cherished forever. Bon, along with Jazz's cousins, held a dupatta over her head as she walked in. Every girl knows that she has to leave her family behind one day and embrace her husband's family. But when the moment actually arrives, it is an overwhelming and emotional time.

'*Vedah shagna da chadiya aao sajanio vedah shagna . . .*'

I heard a Punjabi song come on all of a sudden between the Bollywood dance numbers and I sensed that the moment had arrived. The photographers didn't even care whether I was present and or not. The bride was the star!

There was a rush at the entrance and, as I saw everyone enter, I stood up. My eyes tried seeking her out but too many people obstructed my line of sight. I shifted to get a better look but still couldn't see her. A few minutes later, there she was!

Take a good look at her, Aditya. Look at how beautiful she is in that dress, her hair elegantly done and her face like an angel from above. Take a good look, and remember this moment forever, I thought.

Jazz looked like she was making a considerable effort not to cry. A couple of times she even tried to wipe away a few stray tears until Bon gave her his handkerchief. All eyes were on her as she gracefully glided down the long aisle while I waited for her with a big dorky smile on my face. She walked so elegantly that it was as if she was floating in the air. My eyes brimmed with tears of happiness as I held her hands and lifted her on to the stage. She blushed in a way that I'd never seen before. My heart quickened its pace and, as I unabashedly admired her beauty, she looked at her feet in embarrassment.

Our families joined us then and brought out the rings that had our names engraved on them. Before the ring ceremony began, I signalled to Dipika to bring the bouquet of orchids that she had kept hidden. As she handed it over to me, everyone raised their eyebrows, which, although embarrassing, didn't stop me from proceeding.

I went down on my knees, holding the orchids and said, 'Jazz, I love you. Will you marry me? You are the one with whom I have dreamt of living my entire life. Will you fulfil my dream? You are the one with whom I want to explore the world. Will you allow me to? You have captivated my heart in a manner in which I cannot do a thing other than think and dream of you.'

'Don't you think it's a little late to ask?' Jazz smiled, teasingly, and said, 'Yes! I love you too.'

We hugged and exchanged rings. The moment was captured on camera, but was framed in our hearts. Surpassing all expectations of a long-distance relationship, we had accepted each other completely—our flaws, our mistakes, our imperfections and our differences. Love conquers all, it's true, but it's a different kind of love that only a few know about. True love is filled with compassion, hope, need and trust. And, no matter what, love knows no envy, jealousy, hatred or conflict. I had found that kind of love and she was worth everything to me.

Just as we were about to relax with a glass of wine, the photographer took us outside to click a few candid pictures.

Such a jealous guy! He just wants to keep me away from the wine, I thought but I was glad I could finally have time alone with Jazz, away from our prying guests and families, even if it was to click a few candid photos together. As the photographer got to work, Jazz and I sat on a bench on the lawn in the chilly winter air.

'Can I ask you something?' Without waiting for my reply, Jazz continued. 'Will you change my name after marriage? I heard it's mandatory in Maharashtrian families.'

'I don't think it's mandatory. But I will definitely change yours.'

'Seriously?' She eyed me suspiciously.

'Yes. How about Shantabai?' I gave her a serious look.

'Eww! I might need to start looking for a divorce lawyer.' She laughed.

'Kantabai?'

'Get lost. I'm leaving.'

'Abusing your fiancé? Where are your manners?' I ragged.

'Whatever. Just get lost.'

I held her close and kissed her forehead. 'I was kidding. I am not even going to ask you to change your surname. You can add mine if you want, but it's not a compulsion. I fell in love with Jazz Sethi and you will be the same for me for a lifetime.'

Marriage norms are slightly harsh on the girls I feel— they have to carry the heavy weight of 'Mrs' before their names. It is very difficult for a newly-wed to cope with new responsibilities, get used to a new environment and routine, leaving behind the comfort of their own houses.

'I'll never forget that along with "wife" and "daughter-in-law", you are a "daughter" too!' I said.

'I love you.'

'How quickly you change gears from "get lost" to "love you".'

We inched closer. The photographer was still around and I hoped he was not clicking this part of the story. Our lips were only millimetres away when Jazz suddenly pulled back.

'Remember, you once told me that you'd write a book based on our story? Were you serious?'

What! Where did this come from?

'As long as you don't have a problem with it,' I said, pouting for having missed a kiss.

'So what name will you give your character in the book? Sudeep or Aditya?'

I thought about it for a second, but I already knew.

'Aditya,' I replied.

Acknowledgements

All the people I thank below were my pillars of strength while I was writing the book.

My millions of readers for their unflinching love and support! You mean the world to me.

Jasmine Sethi, my fiancé as I write this, but by the time you read the book, my wife.

Dipika Tanna, my friend who continues to advise me even after my engagement; I still manage to ignore her somehow.

Randeep Randhawa, for pestering Jasmine time and again for letting me pen down this story. I am determined to keep his adventurous ways away from my wedding ceremony.

Madhwi Kapoor and Priyanshi, for making our love story happen. You will stay alive in our memories forever and somewhere in the pages of this book.

Kulwinder Singh Sethi and Tripta Sethi, my parents-in-law and Jasmine's parents, for allowing me to marry their daughter.

I promise to keep their princess not only happy but also give her a life that she desires.

Bonpreet Sethi, my brother-in-law, for playing the role of a catalyst between my in-laws and me! I hope you get married soon so that you too lose ownership of your credit card.

My mom, my dad, my sister, Shweta, and my grandparents, for keeping faith in my work.

Zankrut Oza, for guiding me patiently and for his brotherly love.

God, for being kind to me when it comes to writing.

My extended family on Facebook, Twitter and Instagram who selflessly promote my books.

Milee Ashwarya, Gurveen Chadha, Shruti Katoch and the whole team at Penguin Random House for their patience during the entire writing process.

A Note on the Author

Sudeep Nagarkar has authored seven bestselling novels—*Few Things Left Unsaid*, *That's the Way We Met*, *It Started with a Friend Request*, *Sorry You're Not My Type*, *You're the Password to My Life*, *You're Trending in My Dreams* and *She Swiped Right into My Heart*. He is the recipient of the Youth Achievers Award, and has been featured on the *Forbes India* longlist of the most influential celebrities for three consecutive years. He also writes for television and has given guest lectures in various renowned institutes like the IITs and platforms like TEDx. His books have been translated into various languages, including Hindi, Marathi, Gujarati and Telugu.

Connect with Sudeep via:

Facebook fan page: /sudeepnagarkar

Facebook profile: /nagarkarsudeep

Twitter: @sudeep_nagarkar

Instagram: @sudeepnagarkar

Snapchat: nagarkarsudeep

Website: www.sudeepnagarkar.in